For more than forty years,
Yearling has been the leading name
in classic and award-winning literature
for young readers.

Yearling books feature children's
favorite authors and characters,
providing dynamic stories of adventure,
humor, history, mystery, and fantasy.

Trust Yearling paperbacks to entertain,
inspire, and promote the love of reading
in all children.

OTHER YEARLING BOOKS YOU WILL ENJOY

GIRL OF KOSOVO
Alice Mead

GOODBYE, VIETNAM
Gloria Whelan

BABY
Patricia MacLachlan

BELLE PRATER'S BOY
Ruth White

WHEN ZACHARY BEAVER CAME TO TOWN
Kimberly Willis Holt

ALL THE WAY HOME
Patricia Reilly Giff

BUD, NOT BUDDY
Christopher Paul Curtis

GROVER G. GRAHAM AND ME
Mary Quattlebaum

THE FIRE-EATERS
David Almond

A SINGLE SHARD
Linda Sue Park

The
Mailbox

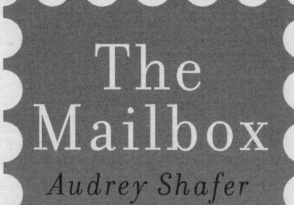

The Mailbox

Audrey Shafer

A YEARLING BOOK

Published by Yearling, an imprint of Random House Children's Books
a division of Random House, Inc., New York

This is a work of fiction. Names, characters, places, and incidents either are the product of
the author's imagination or are used fictitiously. Any resemblance to actual persons, living
or dead, events, or locales is entirely coincidental.

Visit us on the Web! www.randomhouse.com/kids
Educators and librarians, for a variety of teaching tools, visit us at
www.randomhouse.com/teachers

The Library of Congress has cataloged the hardcover edition of this work as follows:

Shafer, Audrey.

The mailbox / Audrey Shafer.

p. cm.

Summary: When twelve-year-old Gabe tries to hide his uncle's death from the local
authorities, he is not prepared for what happens when this secret is discovered.

ISBN: 978-0-385-73344-1 (trade) — ISBN: 978-0-385-90361-5 (lib. bdg.)

[1. Foster home care—Fiction. 2. Uncles—Fiction.] I. Title.

PZ7.S527282Mai 2006

[Fic]—dc22   2006004572

ISBN: 978-0-440-42134-4 (tr. pbk.)
Reprinted by arrangement with Delacorte Press
Printed in the United States of America
August 2008
10 9 8 7 6 5 4 3 2 1
First Yearling Edition

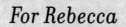

For Rebecca

ACKNOWLEDGMENTS

I would like to thank the veterans whose sacrifices, empathy, and trust inspired this book. I owe much gratitude to my editor, Stephanie Lane, for her wonderful support and insights. Also, without the love and help of my children, family, and friends, this book—and I—would not exist.

The Mailbox

Chapter 1

Vernon Culligan was as good as dead to the town of Drayford, Virginia, for so long that when he actually died, not many folks noticed. For decades, his bloodshot eyes, permanent three-day stubble, rifle held over his head, and snarl meaner than a coon dog's had naturally taught everyone to keep a good distance from his property line. The postal delivery truck did venture all the way to the teetering mailbox, and mail was regularly delivered through its yawning trap into the dark, corrugated steel tunnel. Outgoing letters, mostly bill payments, were collected, the addresses written in shaky black ink, as if little spider legs had grouped themselves into crooked letters. Such was the old man's communication with the world.

Twelve-year-old Gable Culligan Pace lived with his uncle in Vernon's simple home cradled within a valley west of Virginia's Blue Ridge, north of Roanoke County. Gabe had arrived in early spring, two and a half years before. Woodland rhododendrons had splashed their purple heads against spikes of sage green as Gabe whizzed by in the backseat of a social worker's Ford Escort.

Over the space of time and in the shadow of the mountains, Gabe came to appreciate, if not understand, many of Uncle Vernon's habits. For instance, Vernon always kept a fan blowing, no matter the season. He preferred the fan to the cabinet full of smoker's lung medicines. So when Gabe arrived home from school and saw his uncle's electric fan lying on the wooden floor in the study, like a turtle that couldn't right itself, Gabe dropped his backpack at the door. He held his breath and crossed the narrow hall. Vernon's chair lay toppled to one side and Vernon himself lay motionless on the floor, flat on his back.

Gabe had never really touched his uncle, though sometimes he had accidentally brushed Vernon's rough hand while passing the margarine tub or clearing the table. Gabe stood by his uncle's work boots and softly called his name. Vernon, a veteran, had had his left leg amputated below the knee during his final tour in Vietnam, thirty-five years before. But with the latest prosthesis, Vernon walked with barely a limp. "The thing's a chore to get on. Can't *mau len*, can't hurry it up no more, but can't stub my toe, neither!" Gabe saw that the fake foot wasn't angled quite right to the rest of his uncle's body. That twist gave Gabe a little courage. He knelt and touched the plasticized ankle, then moved up, methodically pushing one finger against his uncle's pant leg. He stopped at the thigh, rolled back on his heels, and looked at his uncle's face. Gently he placed a finger on his uncle's cheek.

The skin was cold. Gabe fetched a thick plaid blanket and lay down with his uncle, covering them both. Gabe closed his eyes. Hours later, after dusk had swept the last particles of light from the room, Gabe awoke. He scrambled out from under the blanket, sat hugging his knees on the floor, and cried. Messy crying, the kind of crying that leaves you swollen, red, and leaky. After a while, he snuffled his nose along his arm and sleeve and stared in the direction of the fan. He crawled toward it, fumbled for the switch, and turned it off. The absence of the low rumble startled him. And then he smiled.

Gabe walked into the kitchen, flipped on the light, and fixed himself a peanut butter and honey sandwich. The first bite brought back the first words his uncle ever spoke to him.

"You as skinny as a starved rat. Don't you eat? Come on, let's eat somepin. What'll it be?" Vernon had scowled at Gabe's silence. "Don't tell me they's foisting a dumb one on old Vernon."

When Ms. Rodriguez, the social worker, had nudged Gabe, he'd whispered, "No, sir."

"No, no," answered Vernon. "Let's get one thing straight. I'm no 'sir.' They can save all they's fancy sirs and salutin' for the dress parade. No, life's a jungle,

3

there's no use for sirs in the jungle." Vernon motioned for Gabe to follow him to the kitchen. He laid out different foods on the counter and told Gabe to point to what he liked. Thus the first peanut butter and honey sandwich had been made and eaten under Vernon's roof.

Gabe now carefully cleaned the top of the bear-shaped honey bottle, the way his uncle had taught him. "Clean him right. He don't want no scabby sores atop his head no more'n you do." Then Gabe sat back down at the table and held on to the bear's smooth, golden tummy.

With night pressing its shadows against the windows, and the trees talking night talk, Gabe was not brave enough to go back into his uncle's study. Every evening since he had left the bumpy, eastbound trail of foster care homes and arrived at his uncle's, Gabe would always tell Vernon that he was going to bed.

"G'night, Uncle Vernon."

"Good night, Gabe," his uncle would always reply. Then Vernon would spoon out a ladleful of philosophy like, "Scum-lickin' pus-suckin' buckets of trouble ken happen whether you're good or bad. But why git spit by skunk muck? Stay low and steer clear of screw-ups, Gabe."

Tonight Gabe couldn't bear not hearing his uncle's voice. So he didn't go to bed. Instead, he dozed, on and off, his head on his arms at the kitchen table. In the morning, he changed his shirt and underpants, brushed his teeth, then stood a long time at his uncle's study doorway.

A fly settled on his uncle's cheek and Gabe's eyes widened in terror as the fly walked into his uncle's nostril. Gabe wanted to scream and stamp and change everything there ever was. Maybe he should turn the fan back on. *Maybe Uncle Vernon's been dead a long time and that's why he kept the fan on—to make flies buzz off and hide that he'd been dead for years. No, Gabe, that's crazy thinking—he wasn't dead till yesterday, just turn the fan on. Do it, do it!* Instead, Gabe shocked himself and did something that would later fill him with a shame as thick and fevered as blood. Something he could never undo. Gabe wrenched the fan's cord from the socket, picked up the fan, and threw it down. Again and again. He almost tingled to see the wire frame crumple more and more with each crash. The plastic housing cracked, and pieces scattered across the room. He screamed at the fan and its bits running for cover under the desk and bookcase. "I hate you! You're not allowed to live no more! I'm killing you, you hear? You're dead. Dead! Go away! Go away!"

In his rage, Gabe didn't notice the fly leaving his uncle's nostril until the satisfied insect had made several loops in the air and sat preening its forelegs on the windowsill. Gabe dashed to the window, which normally sat open two inches all through the warm months and couldn't be closed again till winter shrank its wood. The fly escaped just as Gabe, with a mighty, grunting heave, slammed shut the window. He stepped back, surprised at his strength, and looked at his shaking hands. Then he knelt at his uncle's side, carefully tucking the blanket around the body and finally covering his uncle's face and head.

He closed the door to his uncle's study, then grabbed his backpack and ran into the morning, off to his second day of sixth grade.

Chapter 2

"Gable Pace and Kaitlyn Simmons. You are both missing your school forms. You have one more day. Now, be sure your parents complete the forms or you won't be allowed in school."

Gabe hoped he wasn't as red as Kaitlyn. He mumbled a "yessum" to Ms. Tsang, just as two girls, one of whom he knew, twittered behind him. He was at a new school, a middle school that started at sixth grade, and he didn't know all the kids the way he had the previous year. Only about a third of his homeroom class was from his elementary school. His friend Webber was not one of them. Gabe cringed, knowing what would come next.

"How can his parents sign his forms when he hasn't got any?" asked Janet, the girl Gabe knew, as she poked Gabe in the back with a pencil. Ms. Tsang looked flustered by the question and flipped through her files. Then she snapped at the class.

"You're not in grade school anymore, remember. Act responsibly and respect your school. We have a merit and demerit system here. Three demerits and your parents . . ." Here Ms. Tsang stumbled. "And your guardians will be called."

Janet stretched her arm toward the ceiling. She explained that her mother had brought donuts in for the whole sixth grade. "And don't I have the dumb luck to have a summer birthday," complained Janet, "but my mom said I could celebrate today, even though I've been eleven for thirty-four days already."

Three large pastry boxes lay stacked on the corner of Ms. Tsang's desk. Janet was given a hall pass and allowed to distribute boxes to the two other sixth-grade homerooms. By the time she returned, only Gabe hadn't eaten his donut. He was carefully wrapping it in the napkin decorated with the pastry shop logo.

"My donuts aren't good enough for you?" demanded Janet as she flounced into the seat behind him.

Gabe didn't say anything; he just put the donut in an outer pocket of his backpack. He had forgotten to make his lunch and knew lunchtime would be miserable without anything to eat. It was at that moment that Gabe realized he'd had homework for English class. Homework he hadn't done and couldn't possibly do.

"Bring in a book from home—any book will do. It can even be your sister's diary!" Mr. Boehm had joked. Gabe knew that some teachers who joked were the meanest of all, as calculating and teasing as jackals. Joking teachers were either friendly and open, or closed to all but their own humor, in love with their own voice. Gabe hadn't been able to tell in which category Mr. Boehm belonged during the brief class yesterday. And today, Gabe didn't want to find out.

During morning break, Gabe locked himself into a stall of the second-floor boys' bathroom. He pulled out a sheet of paper and tried to imitate his uncle's scritchy cursive:

> Mr. Boehm,
> > No books are allowed from the house.
> > > Respectfully,
> > > Vernon Culligan

Gabe finished just as he heard the rowdy laughter of eighth graders in the next stall and smelled the forbidden tang of burning tobacco. He quickly fled, letting the swinging door of the bathroom flap the jeers away from him. Unfortunately, he ran directly into Ms. Tsang, sniffing the air outside the restrooms. Clutching his backpack in front of him, he could feel the donut flatten with the collision.

"Hold on, Gable, isn't it?"

"Yeah. Gabe."

"What are you boys doing in there?"

"Nothing." Then he added, "Ms. Tsang."

"That nothing certainly is pungent."

She looked him up and down. Suddenly Gabe realized that his brown hair was tangled. His forearms were streaked with grime and his fingernails were dirty and chipped. His navy blue T-shirt was faded to a medium hue and his black canvas pants similarly pounded to a dull gray. *Why is she staring at me?* Gabe knew he was small. Almost all the sixth-grade girls were taller than he was, even Lucinda Liu, who had been a lot shorter than Gabe the previous year. He avoided Ms. Tsang's eyes.

"Do yourself a favor and stay out of trouble. I know *I'm* trying to." She gave a little laugh, and he felt her pat his shoulder with her palm.

The bell rang and Gabe ran to his English class. He meant to give the note to Mr. Boehm before the class started, but once there he stood, unable to decide, just inside the door as the other students filed in. Grinning, Webber ran up and plucked the note from Gabe's hand. It was their first class of the day together.

"Gabey, where've you been? This a note? Here, Mr. Boehm!" Webber handed the note to the teacher and led his friend to the back row. "Look, I want to warn you. I got the lowdown on some stuff after school yesterday. Whatever you do, don't use the bathroom on the second floor. It's *owned* by eighth graders. And the teachers watch it like hawks. Also, there's no video shack in the basement. So don't let anyone sell you a video pass."

The boys sat down and glanced up at the front of the room. Mr. Boehm was tall and slender with a short spiky haircut and a pale brown goatee. He gave Gabe a searching look as he refolded the note with his long fingers, placed it on his desk, and tapped it absently.

"Settle into your seats. If you talk with your neighbor, he or she will no longer be your neighbor. Everything you say in this room is for the whole class, including me. I am interested in your minds!"

The students giggled as Mr. Boehm swept his pointing finger at them and laughed a low *ha-ah!* Gabe was just about to place his English teacher in the "jackal" category when Mr. Boehm continued.

"I want to tell you something very important now. If you learn nothing else from me the entire year but this one thing, then I've done my job. Any guesses?"

Hands were raised and suggestions offered. "Do your homework!" "Don't be late!" "Always raise your hand!" "Don't interrupt the teacher!" "Pay attention!" "No cheating!"

Mr. Boehm gave an exaggerated sigh and called on Anneka.

"Always write neatly and try your best and neatness counts and—"

"Thank you. Now, Webber."

"Don't eat poo!"

Mr. Boehm gave Webber a stern look, then called on Janet.

"Don't eat a hippopotamus!"

During all of this, Gabe had quietly slipped a book from a back shelf of the room. He rarely spoke in class and never volunteered an answer. When his name was called, he would hesitate, then respond briefly and quietly, as if hoping the search beacon would swiftly pass. The book he held in his hands was *Of Mice and Men.* He liked the title instantly, and held the book on his lap, hidden behind his backpack. He felt the tempting peel of the pages, opened the book, and started to read.

"No, you're all completely, utterly, unbelievably wrong," Mr. Boehm was saying. "The most wrong answers I have ever heard. You have outdone yourselves with wrongness. A Fullerton Middle School record for wrongness. But there is one boy here with the right answer."

"Webber?" said Janet, to loud guffaws.

"No," replied Mr. Boehm. "The boy next to Webber."

Everyone turned to Gabe, who, startled from the scene on the riverbank, slapped the book closed.

"Gabe has the answer. So he gets a merit for today."

Gabe's tongue was plastered stiff and dry to the roof of his mouth. He watched Mr. Boehm return to his desk, pull a white merit slip from his drawer, write briefly on it, then hold it up as if to read a proclamation.

"On second thought, Gabe, you do the honors."

Mr. Boehm strode to Gabe's seat and handed him the paper. Gabe swallowed, trying to draw some moisture into his mouth.

"Merit awarded to Gabe Pace," Gabe rasped. "English 6A. Mr. Boehm. For knowing that books are your friends, through thick and thin, no matter what."

"Aw, that's cinchy—I could have told you that!"

"Ah, but Charley," Mr. Boehm replied. "You didn't."

To Gabe's relief, Mr. Boehm left him alone for the rest of the period. Volunteers were requested to show books

from home, class workbooks and readers were distrib-
uted, a spelling list was dictated, and attendance was
taken. As the bell rang, Mr. Boehm reminded his students: "Any book you take from this room must first be
signed out with me."

Webber left for PE, and Gabe found himself as unsure
as he'd felt at the beginning of class. He had already put
the novel back on the shelf, but his fingers twitched.

"You know, Gabe, I've already marked you down for
the book. You might as well take it with you."

"Thank you," Gabe mumbled. He slipped the book
into his pack and scurried from the room.

For the rest of the day Gabe wondered how Mr. Boehm
understood that the only minutes of the day when Gabe's
head was not near exploding with the image of his uncle's
body were the few moments he had spent in the book with
George and Lennie, drinking from the green pool. As the
hours passed, Gabe felt his chance to tell someone about
Uncle Vernon crumble and sift through his fingers, until
all he had left was a stain, a shadow. Maybe it didn't even
happen. *But it did!* He felt battered by questions. Why
didn't he get someone right away? An ambulance? How
did he know his uncle was dead, anyway? Maybe they
would think Gabe had killed him! Like the time at the
third foster home—the fire! *Remember that!* Everyone suspicious of Gabe, the newcomer. Gabe "conveniently" vol-
unteering to help after school that day. *Sure!* Foster kids
don't do that around here, he was told. *Wise up!* And he
had liked that foster mother so much—he had wanted to
impress her, to make her want to keep him. He didn't like

starting new schools in new towns every eight to ten months. But that incident did at least lead him to Vernon. Gabe's file finally rose to the top; his mother's older half brother, born in western Virginia, had been located.

Fingering his pancaked donut, Gabe caught himself muttering aloud in the play yard, "But I didn't kill him." Fortunately no one heard, not even Webber, who, after giving half his sandwich to his friend, had left to buy a snack. Webber's movements were jerky and restless until a ball was in sight. Then his muscles and rhythms lent even his sixth-grade strut a certain grace. Webber returned, tossing and catching his bag of chips, just as the bell signaled the end of lunch.

By the time school ended, Gabe was exhausted and limped onto the public bus. The bus stop was close—right across the street from school. But at the other end of his ride, a long walk awaited him. His uncle's house, built in a hollow at the end of a twisting, poorly paved road, lay in a pocket between two otherwise adjacent towns. Vernon had, in his heyday, angrily fought any changes that affected his property. After a while the two towns just ignored Vernon and his property. Street lighting was out of date, and the road didn't drain properly during major downpours. Vernon's house was small, almost hidden by the surrounding elm, ash, maple, hickory, and spruce trees. A stately chestnut tree crowned the leafy glade.

Gabe walked more and more slowly down Lapan Lane. Two houses flanked the entrance to the lane; then there was nothing till Vernon's property. Gabe waited at the mailbox and gazed at the towering trees. He was stalling and he knew it. His uncle was always the mail collector. Although Gabe did just about every other chore—made bank deposits and withdrawals, shopped for groceries and took out trash, even bought stamps at the post office—his uncle always opened and emptied the mailbox. Gabe bit his lip, then opened the arched mailbox door. Sometimes, Gabe knew from watching his uncle return empty-handed from the box, there was no mail. Today the box held one letter.

Gabe turned the letter over and over. No stamp. He looked around but only met the eye of a squirrel parked midway up a nearby trunk. The envelope was deep green, the lettering in white. "To: Mr. G.C.P.," it read. Gabe could feel his heart pound, sharp and cold. The envelope was not sealed, just the flap tucked, as for an invitation. Inside was a single cream white card, with the following sentence in flowing script:

I have a secret.

He turned the card over and read, written in the same elegant hand:

Do not be afraid.

Gabe was more afraid than ever. He looked back down the lane but could see no one. Carefully he stepped to the house. He opened the front door and softly laid down his pack. He turned on every light, then gently opened the door to the study.

His uncle's body, leg prosthesis and all, was gone.

Chapter 3

Gabe trembled as he stood in the doorway. He wanted—
what? What did he wish for at that moment? Perhaps he
should have wished for time to step backward and plunk
him in the past, his uncle wheezing and pacing between
backyard trees. Or even further back, to Gabe's earliest
years, when he could be comforted and carried securely
on the hip of his mother. But he couldn't remember those
years, and he wasn't thinking very clearly. What he wished
for was to be magically transformed into Webber.

He did the next best thing.

He pretended to be Webber.

"Whoa-ho!" said Gabe-Webber. "What do we have

here? Nothing interesting. What losers! No baseballs. No music. No music, man! No computer! Just an old pencil holder. And what's this? A phone that doesn't even work? Dark Ages! There's got to be something here!"

Gabe-Webber sat in Vernon's desk chair, spinning it. But when the chair whirled over the part of the floor that had held Vernon's body, Gabe smashed his feet to the floor so abruptly that he fell. For Gabe, the floor still held the imprint of his uncle, like the outline drawn in white at the scene of a murder-mystery crime.

Gabe's image of himself as Webber popped like a balloon. Nevertheless, he felt a little better now that he was kneeling on the floor, rubbing his palms, which had been scraped by the tumble. Something white caught his eye. Something shiny, stuck just behind a front leg of the bookcase. He crept toward it and wiggled it out with two fingers.

He held one of the rectangular plastic buttons from his uncle's fan. A small chip was missing from one corner, but it was otherwise intact. He stared at it, then looked around the room once more. Yes, not only was his uncle missing, but so were the broken fan and the blanket. Clutching his find, Gabe rolled to his feet and walked to the center of the house. The doors to both bedrooms were ajar, and, leaning this way and that, Gabe could see that his uncle's bed was empty. And his own was almost empty, except for the thick plaid blanket neatly folded in the center.

Gabe crept to his room, sliding one hand along the wall. He pushed his door all the way open with his foot.

16

A sandwich and a bottle of apple juice waited for him on the corner of his desk closest to his bed. He sat on the edge of his bed, away from the blanket, and laid the button on his desk. He ate the sandwich, the peanut butter and honey just right. He popped open the juice, drank it, then picked up the button again. He was about to get into bed but remembered something. After retrieving the cream-colored card from the hallway floor where he had dropped it with his pack, he propped it against the juice bottle. He set it so he could see the words "Do not be afraid." Then he unfolded the blanket, curled his legs under it, and, lying on his side, with one hand under his pillow, fisted around the plastic button, he fell asleep.

Always a restless sleeper, Gabe awoke early the next morning, the blanket bunched at the foot of the bed and the pillow tipped into the dust between his bed and desk. The tease of predawn gave his room a ghostly glow, and he was glad he had left the hall lights on—something his uncle would never allow. "Crab it all, Gabe, it ain't Christmas!" he would have grumped. Gabe wiped the drool from the side of his mouth and blinked at the card. *Do not be afraid.* He rose and wandered into the bathroom, then the kitchen.

Gabe hoped his fairy godmother, as he now believed the card writer to be, would have made him breakfast as well. But the kitchen was untouched, and Gabe slopped some cereal flakes and milk into a bowl. The crunch of his chewing seemed loud, and every so often he would stop, mid-grind, to listen for other sounds. Larks and sparrows, warblers and tufted titmice announced the coming day; otherwise, the air was silent. At one point Gabe raced back to his bedroom and picked up not only the card, but also the plastic fan button, which had fallen with the pillow. He shoved the button into his pants pocket.

Once morning had fully whisked night away, Gabe explored the house. "Halloo, fairy godmother, are you in there?" he asked of every cranny and turn. He avoided the gun case under his uncle's bed but stopped for a moment before his uncle's closet and breathed in deeply. He fingered the few shirts his uncle owned and noticed, with a jolt, Vernon's foot-and-leg prosthesis standing guard in a murky corner. The straps hung down in loops like an old man's suspenders, and the cushioned sleeve at the top sagged like a yellowed undershirt. Gabe closed the door and entered the front room—the only room with a clear view of the mailbox.

Gabe sat at the window, waiting for his miracle. The mysterious card writer could, he was certain, teleport him to a sun-and-rainbow land just as surely as she had blinked away his uncle's body. She would be plump and have a twinkle in her eye. She would wear an apron and have very tiny feet that she didn't really need as she fluttered in midair. Gabe could almost smell the cinnamon-roll aroma that wisped around her.

Suddenly Gabe realized that his fairy godmother might have already left another note for him, and he sprang from the bench and raced to the mailbox. But no, it was empty. He walked once around the house, kicked stones and tossed a stick, then returned to wait by the windowsill.

What did school matter anymore? If he had been home yesterday, he would have been taken along with his uncle. He couldn't miss her today.

He amused himself with tapping on his knee to check his reflex, as the doctor had done during his last school physical. Then he tapped all over his body to see if any other place caused a jerk. He watched some squirrels through the window. He made a print of his hand on the glass.

Waiting was boring.

What if she was invisible? Huh, he hadn't thought of that. Maybe she was in a different dimension. Maybe that was her secret. *Maybe she's an alien and only pretending to be a fairy godmother. Maybe she really looks more like a squid, with lots of tentacles, and she isn't cozy at all. And she's an it, not a she.* Gabe shivered and rubbed the plastic button in his pocket. He wished he were bored again. Instead, he was nervous, and the next time he checked the mailbox, he opened the latch hesitantly, as if a moray eel would lunge from the box and snatch him. But again, the box was empty.

Now what? He didn't want to be at home. He should have gone to school. He checked the clock in the kitchen—almost afternoon. What if he just left? Hmm. He could pack a little bag and head out. Travel light. Catch trains. But no, he knew even as he started his mental journey that he could never do that. Hulking images of stone-faced truant officers crowded his vision—and clicking red finger-nails of case workers and police with guns in thick black leather holsters—yes, he would be shuffled into a police lineup, wanted for murder!

Even school sounded better than being led away in handcuffs. Gabe opened his backpack to look at his schedule. *Let's see.* Eleven-fifteen. English was just over. Webber would have rushed off to PE.

Gabe reached deep into his backpack and pulled out the Steinbeck book. *A book is a friend, no matter what.* No, that wasn't quite right. Gabe opened his English folder and reread his merit slip. Three times. He smiled and took his book into his bedroom to read the first chapter. He liked Lennie a lot. And the rabbits. That would be fun, to have rabbits. Gabe rolled off his bed and squatted before his shelf. He didn't have many toys, but he had some. A few trucks. A toy gun. A pack of cards, some missing. A defuzzed tennis ball. Rooting behind a collection of rocks, he found it. A little blue bunny that Webber's mother had given Gabe last Easter. He rubbed the bunny against his cheek. *I'd let you have this, Lennie, if you wanted it. I wouldn't let George take it away.*

Holding his stuffed bunny and his book, Gabe went into the kitchen to search for a can of beans. He wanted Lennie to know that some people ate beans without ketchup. Gabe knelt on the counter and emptied the cupboard of every last can but found no beans. He pretended the floor swarmed with writhing black snakes, and he heated a can of tomato rice soup without leaving the counter, reaching down so low for the pot in the bottom

20

cupboard that he had to curl his toes around the sink spigot to keep from falling.

The scrape of the wooden spoon on the warming pot stirred more than the soup. Uncle Vernon's voice rose from Gabe's memory.

"Don't believe everything they tell you, boy. A watched pot does boil and sometimes you ken tell a book by its cover. Why, iffen there's a naked lady on it, then it ain't gonna show up in no Sunday school class, now is it? And take me, for instance. I ain't gonna show up in no Sunday school class, neither." Gabe had smiled at this speech, but when his uncle demanded a reason for the grin, Gabe had lowered his head.

Tired of the snakes game, Gabe ate his soup at the kitchen table. And read. He took breaks from reading, though, and watched the mail truck, with its squat perkiness, stop in front of the box. The mail lady smartly flipped open the box, and Gabe waited several minutes for the departing rumble of the truck to fade. Then he took the bunny and checked the mailbox once more. There were two envelopes addressed in type to Vernon Culligan, 13 Lapan Lane. One from the electric company, with a cellophane window. The other, from VFW Honor Veterans Every Day, sported a tiny American flag printed to the left of Vernon's name. Gabe placed the mail on the outermost corner of his uncle's study desk and fled the room and the house.

Gabe swung from the tire he and his uncle had hung in the backyard the previous spring. Vernon had firmly believed in fixing and making do. "A man's gotta master

21

knots or he may as well swing from one." As a reward for learning the square, bowline, weaver's hitch, double fisherman's, hangman's noose, all manner of hitches, and suchlike, Gabe got to choose what he wanted to make with a knot. He looked silently at his chafed hands. "Whatsa matter, no imagination?" Vernon had said. Gabe still hadn't replied. Truth was, he had wanted a hammock, but he wasn't used to voicing his desires. "Okay, Gabe. Here's a list. You stop me when I say somepin interesting. A rope ladder. A lariat. Model riggin'. A tire swing—" Yes, Gabe had said excitedly. That's it. A tire swing. The next day, after Gabe had returned from school, there lay a rope and a tire in the back, ready for him. With his uncle's directions, generously laced with cussing, Gabe secured the rope to the chestnut's outstretched limb and then to the tire. He liked to lie back in the swing, once he got it going, his hands fastened over the knot, and stare at the leaves rushing overhead. A tire swing was better than a hammock.

Everything Gabe touched seemed to choke out his uncle's words. As soon as he climbed into the swing, he heard his uncle's praise and the pink feeling it had given him. "Now, that's a job well done, Gabe. You ken be proud of that one."

After swinging a long time, Gabe rechecked the mailbox. It was after the time he would have been home from school. He even banged his hand around inside the empty box. Then he returned to the house, to his room, and read his book. It took him a while to finish. And then he read the end again. He looked mournfully at his little blue bunny, which had fallen to its side like a stiff wooden soldier. *George is mean,* he thought. *And Lennie never had a chance.*

And that was when Gabe knew. If Lennie didn't have a fairy godmother, neither did he.

Chapter 4

Gabe remembered to bring a note of excused absence but forgot all about the official school papers when he returned the following day. Kaitlyn had remembered hers. When questioned by Ms. Tsang, Gabe stammered that he must have lost the papers. She directed him to the school office, and he used morning break to stand in various lines and collect copies from harassed office workers and parent volunteers. Hence, he arrived at Mr. Boehm's class flustered and late. He slipped into the seat Webber had saved for him at the back.

Everyone had already taken out a sheet of loose-leaf paper, narrow-lined, for the spelling quiz. In his hurry to locate his binder, Gabe accidentally spilled the blue bunny from his backpack. The bunny bounced a few feet and landed at the base of Janet's chair.

"Aw, how cute!" she exclaimed. "Somewone bwought their wittle wabbit fwend to school-y wool-y today."

Gabe's stomach churned as the bunny was tossed from student to student and laughter sharpened the air. Mr. Boehm snatched the bunny from the game.

"That is quite enough. The next person to make a comment gets a demerit. Now, who lays claim to this animal?"

Silence greeted him. Finally Webber said, "It's mine, Mr. Boehm."

Mr. Boehm glared at a snickering student, turned to Webber, and then faced the rest of the class. "That's fine. I'll have it here for you at the end of the class. Now, everyone, ready? The first word is 'malicious.' Malicious."

The students huddled over their papers and by the end of the period, Webber, forgetting about the bunny, ran off to his favorite class. Gabe waited, pretending to retie his sneaker laces while Anneka batted her eyes and asked Mr. Boehm a long question about the writing assignment. At last she left and Mr. Boehm looked at Gabe.

"Here it is," he said, handing the bunny to Gabe.

"Thanks," Gabe mumbled.

"Good friends are rare. I was even tempted to give Webber a merit." Gabe didn't say anything, so Mr. Boehm asked, "Do you think George was a good friend to Lennie?"

Gabe hesitated. Then he spoke slowly. "You need more than books for friends. The stable hand, Crooks—he knows that." Gabe laid the book on Mr. Boehm's desk and ran from the room.

Gabe's next class, math, was just down the hall. Janet and her pal Brooke huddled together; their giggling grew louder when Gabe rushed by. He felt his ears burn and ignored the girls even though they bumped and burbled directly behind him into the classroom.

The seats were assigned in math class. Mrs. Garvey, a no-nonsense African American teacher with clear gray eyes, designed the seating plan so that friends never sat together. Janet's seat was right next to Gabe's. Why couldn't his schedule match Webber's? Why did he have to have nearly every class with Janet? Janet liked math, had a flair for word problems and puzzles, and could frequently answer questions when her classmates were stumped. Her ease with numbers subdued her usual scarlet-loud, attention-demanding style. She always wore a lock of her tawny red hair plaited into a narrow braid that hung, with a glow-in-the-dark plastic bead at the end, along the side of her face. When she was deep in thought in math class, Gabe noticed she would twiddle the braid with the index finger of her left hand. He liked that. He thought Lennie would like that too.

When the bell rang, Gabe was still carefully writing down Mrs. Garvey's last statement about decimals and percents. Janet, having quickly crammed her books into her pack to rush to lunch period, reconsidered and sat back down.

"Do you get it?" she asked Gabe.

"Huh? Uh, no, not really," he replied sheepishly.

"It's like this. Percent always means percent of something. It doesn't mean much on its own. So if you have four apples and I take all of them, that is, I take a hundred percent of your apples, then I'll have four. But if you have six apples, and I take a hundred percent, then I'd have six apples. You have to multiply by one for a hundred percent, and point five for fifty percent, and so on. Do you get it now?"

"Sorta. Yeah, that helps." He felt as dumb as Lennie.

She shrugged. "I'm going to lunch. You forget yours again?"

Gabe flinched. What, did she watch him all the time? "No," he replied. "I got it."

He carefully packed his math books into his backpack so that she wouldn't see the stuffed animal. She gave up waiting and ran out the door, calling to a friend in the jammed hallway.

"Jeez, Gabe, whatcha been doing? You're late all the time." Webber waited for Gabe at their spot—the end of the farthest lunch table.

"Sorry. Hey, thanks for sticking up for me in English."

"What?" Webber had forgotten the incident. "Oh yeah, that. It was nothing. I got one of those at home too, you know. So it wasn't really lying. Anyway, forget it. The important thing is, did Uncle V say you can come over on Saturday?"

Gabe considered the question carefully. Then he said, "I'm allowed to sleep over now."

Webber let loose a whoop. "Wow! That's great! I'll ask my mom but I know what she'll say." Webber imitated his mother's slight Southern accent. "Ring the bells and call the preacher. It's about time!"

Though he was relieved that Webber had not asked what, exactly, had changed Vernon's opinion, Gabe still felt his throat tighten. Not so much because of the thickening pile of paper lies that the school demanded of him, but because of skirting the truth with his friend. The last thing Gabe wanted, the very last thing, was to get Webber in trouble. He couldn't tell his friend. He couldn't even slip up a little.

Webber constantly danced at the edge of detention for misbehavior—clowning, running when he wasn't allowed to run, playing minor pranks. He not only liked attention, he craved it. They had found each other at the end of third grade—Gabe, ever the new kid, and Webber the goof. Webber was tall and had a shock of curly dirty blond hair. You instantly knew when Webber entered a room—even the air seemed to bounce from the walls when he was around. Webber was almost thirteen years old, and Gabe was barely twelve.

Gabe wished Mr. Boehm had given Webber a merit—Gabe could picture Mrs. Pickering taping it to the refrigerator door. Gabe liked Mrs. Pickering, the way she pursed her lips before she said, "Do come into my office," and pointed to the kitchen. She was as cheery as the clink of a spoon in a teacup, but too busy to sit still for teatime. She operated a home-baked pie business—Pickering Pies. The kitchen was always crusty-warm, as enveloping as a Mrs. Pickering hug. Gabe couldn't wait till he would say "G'night" to Mrs. Pickering and she would say "Good night" back.

Webber slapped Gabe on the arm. "Come on, quit daydreaming. Let's go play Horse."

The two boys ran off to play basketball. Webber excelled at sports and became fiercely competitive at games. His only friend who didn't feel threatened by this drive was Gabe. So even though Webber had a large circle of friends—classmates who laughed at his jokes and teammates from basketball, Little League, swimming, and soccer—Gabe was special to Webber. Gabe usually spent Saturday afternoons at the Pickerings' if Webber wasn't at his father's. Webber was almost Gabe's coach—he had taught Gabe tricks of dribbling, passing, shooting, and connecting with the ball.

"Webber," said Gabe suddenly.

"Yeah." Webber made his shot, then looked at Gabe.

"You remember when you taught me to swim?" Gabe asked.

"Kinda. No, not really. That was a long time ago."

Two summers earlier, as a guest at the swim club, Gabe would sit, dry as a stick, in hand-me-down trunks from Webber, watching the swim team. Gabe liked looking at the light on the surface of the water, or the white foam chopped up by a racer's arms or legs. Mrs. Pickering would ask him if he wanted to swim, but he always said no.

"Gabe-man, come on, try that shot. You're mooning all over the place."

29

"I was just thinking that now, if that happened, I would tell you."

"If what happened? You're not making any sense."

"You know, if I was so close to the edge I could fall in the water . . ."

One sweltering August day, Webber had told Gabe he wanted to show him something on the side of the pool. Gabe had cautiously leaned over the edge to see where Webber pointed. After Webber pushed him in, he had sunk steadily. Gabe could feel his hair spike out from his head, and he spread his arms to pretend he was in a spaceship. He had wondered why he was so afraid of water—it was like being inside a big blue box of coolness. Until he couldn't breathe. He'd thrashed his arms and legs but couldn't get any closer to the sky wavering above him. The water had been pierced by a streak—Webber had grabbed Gabe's flailing arm and pulled him to the surface. He'd put Gabe's hand on the edge and held up his friend. The lifeguard had rushed over, Mrs. Pickering not far behind. Gabe had gulped air, and when the lifeguard had asked him what'd happened, he'd said he'd fallen in. The lifeguard had told him to be more careful and returned to her post.

"Look, dopey, why didn'tcha tell me," Webber had said. "I'm teaching you to swim right now."

Webber had helped Gabe walk the wall hand-over-hand to the shallow end and had begun the first lesson. From that moment on, Webber had been Gabe's protector.

Webber sank another basket and protested: "But if you fell in a pool, you'd swim to the side."

"Yeah, you're right. Forget it."

The bell clanged—Webber had won at Horse twice already—and they parted for afternoon classes. As Gabe turned to get his backpack, he noticed Janet and Brooke scurrying away from the table. They giggled as usual, heads glued together like a double-knobbed clothespin. He looked around, then checked to see if the three items he had stowed in his backpack were still present: the bunny, the plastic button, and the card. All were accounted for and, as far as he could tell, untouched.

Gabe dragged through the rest of the day. Being back at school made him realize how lonely he would be at home. He entered Ms. Tsang's art room, his last class on Thursday. She explained the still-life arrangement.

" 'Memento mori' means 'remember that you will die.' Painters put these reminders next to fruit or flowers or even lobsters. Signs of nature, of life, that will eventually die."

"But Ms. Tsang. That skull is plastic. Plastic never dies."

Janet, of course.

Gabe drooped at the shoulders. Maybe Saturday and his trip to Webber's would come quickly. Then he realized that Monday was a holiday—Labor Day. He laid his pencil next to his drawing and put his head on his arms. If only he would get appendicitis right now! Like Lucinda last year. She'd had a stomachache one afternoon, and by the next morning she'd had an operation. Everyone had been required to decorate a big card for her. Larger than the teacher's desk blotter. Yes, appendicitis would be good.

He could be in a hospital, and nurses with soft fingers and damp cloths would take care of him. Gabe sat up abruptly. No, he couldn't get sick. Then they'd find out and take him away and he'd never see Webber again. Gabe studiously peered at the still life displayed at the front of the class and set his pencil to work.

After school ended, Gabe stared from the window as the bus wound through the town and finally wheezed to his stop. He trudged off the bus and plodded toward Lapan Lane. Once home, he again paused at the mailbox. He looked up at the clouds collecting and thickening, graying the sky like scum on a pond. He sighed and swung down the box's door. Two letters waited: one a thin letter for Vernon Culligan from Fullerton Middle School; the other an unstamped deep green envelope addressed, in delicate script, to Mr. G.C.P.

Chapter 5

Gabe frowned as he held the green envelope. He had a habit of working his tongue inside his cheek when he worried. Maybe he should just go to the police now. They would understand. Jeez, he was just a kid, as Webber would say.

Gabe pulled the card from the envelope.

I want to help you.

He flipped the card over.

You are the best thing to ever happen to Vernon.

Then in the tiniest of script were words that Gabe had to squint to read:

P.S. The dog's name is Guppy.

Wow! A dog! Gabe ran to the house, threw open the front door, and dropped his belongings. The door to his bedroom stood wide open. There, lying on the thick plaid blanket, was a very large black dog. As Gabe stared, the dog rose. "G-good dog," Gabe managed to whisper. "Good Guppy. Stay. Stay." The dog cocked its head to one side and pricked its flopped ears at their folds. Gabe said, "Down, Guppy." To his relief, the dog lay down, its head up and its eyes on Gabe. Gabe cautiously walked to his room and stood in the doorway.

"Hi, Guppy. I'm Gabe." The dog rolled onto its side. Gabe approached his bed and let Guppy sniff his hand. When Guppy licked his palm, Gabe ran his hand down the length of Guppy's body. Then he wrapped his arms tightly around the dog's neck. He rubbed Guppy's tummy and discovered that Guppy was a girl. Gabe ran the thin black velvet of her ears over his hands and across his cheek. She gave a couple of sneezes and tail thumps of appreciation. Gabe especially liked the thick ruff of fur behind Guppy's head, down the back of her neck, and between her shoulders. He could lose his hands there, then pull his fingers up, like pink fish rising from a bed of soft seaweed. He put his nose into her fur. She smelled a little funny, sort of like—a gas station? The fabric store Mrs. Pickering had taken him to once? Maybe it was flea powder. Bellbottom, the Pickerings' cat, required flea dips to hold off mange. And Guppy didn't have a flea collar. Or any collar. Should she have a collar?

Gabe didn't know much about dogs. But he knew he loved Guppy. Instantly.

"Good bo—" Gabe caught himself. "Good girl, Guppy."

Guppy followed Gabe to the bathroom. "No, Guppy, you stay here." To his delight, Guppy waited outside the bathroom door. After he came out, Gabe said, "Come on, girl, let's get something to eat. Do you like honey and peanut butter?" She was so tall that he could still pet her behind the ears as they walked together. Her face was long and narrow, her eyes alert and copper brown, and she held her shaggy wolflike tail in a long, shallow U.

A huge bag of dog food leaned against the side of the refrigerator. The label said, "For large dogs."

"Cool," said Gabe.

He also found two heavy ceramic bowls on the floor. Guppy slurped water from one, then licked the floor. Gabe lifted the other and removed the cream-colored card.

She needs two cups every morning and
evening. No other food.
If you are gone for a night, give her extra before
you go.
She drinks a lot of water.
I left the dog door for you to finish.

Dog door? Gabe flipped the card over, but there were no more instructions. The kitchen opened onto the back of

35

the property. Sure enough, a rectangular hole had been sawed in the door, as well as screw holes. The dog door itself, with its heavy plastic flap, lay against the counter. Gabe squealed and crawled through the hole in the door. He stuck his head back in and called, "Come, Guppy, come on!" Guppy bounded for the door and squeezed through. She and Gabe ran and jumped and raced and played and drank the humid swag of summer air between the trees. Her tongue hung from the side of her mouth and her ears flopped and streamed when she charged full gallop after a stick. Gabe couldn't remember ever being so happy. So happy that he sank to his knees and wrapped his arms around her panting body and cried into her black, black warmth.

Once inside, Gabe remembered to refill Guppy's water bowl, which she emptied right away. He crawled back out the door hole to get a screwdriver from Uncle Vernon's toolshed. Guppy followed him everywhere. As he eased open the shed's old wooden door, he could hear his uncle.

"What? Don't know a pipe wrench from needle-nose pliers? A sledgehammer from a ball-peen? Goodness, Gabe, you's a mess!" Gabe imitated Vernon for Guppy's benefit.

Vernon had taught Gabe all the names, let him feel the heft of each tool—how to hold and angle each. He'd even taught Gabe how to use a power drill and a radial saw. When Gabe had told Webber about that lesson, Webber had burned with envy. His father didn't even think he should use scissors! Webber had punched Gabe and called him a liar. "I am not a liar!" Gabe had screamed back, rubbing his shoulder. It was one of their few fights. "You are too!" Webber had yelled. "A big fat"—Webber had paused, laughing good-naturedly—"screwball hammerhead." Gabe had allowed himself a little snort.

"Okay, and you're a . . . a Phillips head and I'm gonna socket to ya." They wound up giddy with laughter over Webber's imitation of someone repeatedly hitting his thumb with a hammer. Nonetheless, when Vernon gave Gabe his own toolbox for his twelfth birthday, Gabe didn't tell Webber. It was this toolbox, with his own screwdriver, that Gabe took from the shed.

Working on the dog door, Gabe chatted to his new friend. "You know, Gup. I am a big fat liar. Not about tools. But Webber's right about me now. I hope you don't mind." Guppy lay with front paws forward and her long snout between them on the black and white checked floor. She watched the operation with, it seemed to Gabe, intense interest and inquiring eyes. "Yes, and you know what else? Uncle Vernon would be real mad at me. Seeing the tools reminded me. 'Gabe'—that's Uncle Vernon talking—'a pig used ta living in mud woulda packed his bags and cleared outta this slobby armpit.' That's what he would say, all right. I'm gonna clean up right after I'm finished here. So you can be proud of living in a nice clean house."

Scattered from kitchen to bedroom were all the dishes and pots Gabe had used since Monday; bits of food sprouted mold and crusted in various states of decay. Islands of dirty clothes pocked his bedroom floor, and squirts of toothpaste dotted the bathroom sink like pastel blue slugs. The mysterious card writer might have been interested in helping Gabe, but that aid did not include daily housekeeping.

Gabe finished the dog door, and he and Guppy both tried it out. Gabe returned his toolbox to the shed. Then he sat down with Guppy for a face-to-face serious lesson.

"You're never to run away. You hear me? I'll always come back. You have to, too. You can do whatever else you want. But you have to promise you'll never leave me. Okay? Okay, Guppy?"

Guppy didn't say anything. Just looked at Gabe with her head tilted.

"All right, Gup, just to make sure, I'm gonna take your paw and sh—"

Before Gabe could finish his sentence, the dog had raised a front paw. Gabe grabbed it and shook it, crying with delight. *Yes, yes, she'll never run away. She understands!*

The setting sun cast a muted orange glow through the cloud bank. Leaves exposed their pale underbellies in the rising breezes and insects hummed their frantic songs. Once inside, the boy fixed their suppers, cleaned and tidied. Then he sat at his desk and did his homework. Guppy, stretched out, covered about two-thirds of the bed. As he worked, Gabe educated Guppy on decimals and percents (as far as he understood such things), the ancient culture of Mesopotamia, and the attractive and repellent features of magnetic poles. He saved English for last. Gabe heaved a sigh and wrote the assigned essay topic at the top of his page: "What I Want Most in This World." He added "by Gabe Pace" and the date. Then he stopped.

How could he write what he wanted most? That he wanted to say goodnight to his uncle and know he'd be there in the morning, catching the dawn's breeze with his fan. Even Mr. Boehm was forcing Gabe to lie! It wasn't fair! He drummed his pencil on his desk and kicked his feet against the legs of his chair. In the middle of his explaining his problem to Guppy, and his need to keep her a secret too, she rose, stretched, and left the room. Gabe heard the *phumf* of the dog door. He was anxious until she returned, when he sprinkled her fur, damp from the first drops of rain, with kisses of relief. Back at his desk, he studied the cards from the mysterious writer, the plastic button, and the blue bunny. Then he worked on his essay. He wrote steadily, though slowly. Guppy's sturdy breathing helped him concentrate and settled his nervous twitches.

By the time Gabe put down his pencil, rain pelted his bedroom window, and he gazed at spattered drops racing down the glass. One little drop sat by itself in a corner of the pane. Gabe rose and tapped the glass over it. But no other drops landed nearby, and it remained alone, unable to join the others slip-sliding in their watery paths.

Gabe picked up the three cream-colored cards. He flipped and twirled them as if they were dancing partners, and marched them on the desk single file. Then he pulled out another piece of loose-leaf paper and wrote:

Dear Mystery Card Writer,
Thank you for Guppy.
I love her.
                    Gabe
P.S. Who are you?

He quickly folded the paper and wrote "To: Mystery Card Writer" on the outside. Gabe turned out his light and climbed into bed with Guppy. He curled his body around hers and nuzzled her neck. Her damp fur smelled like ink and trampled leaves mixed together. He murmured to her, and for the first time that week, he did not wake up, sweating and panting, choking on the gray veil of night.

The next morning Gabe held another serious powwow with Guppy. No leaving now. He wished he hadn't told Webber he would sleep over Saturday night. But the card writer seemed to know Gabe would do something like that. Gabe got up and put two extra bowls of water down on the floor. He remembered that Monday would be a holiday and excitedly told the news to Guppy. *A whole day! Just you and me!* Guppy thumped and wagged and discovered a very itchy area on her side to scratch with her big rabbity back paw.

Before leaving for school, Gabe solemnly opened the rusty mailbox. Heavy drops of the night's rain fell from the latch onto his wrist. He checked that the inside was dry and left his note in the middle of the cold metal floor.

Chapter 6

It was Friday morning, and Gabe scrunched into the farthest corner of the back bench on the nearly empty bus. No other schoolmates rode the 42 bus from as far away as Gabe's neighborhood, but plenty would climb aboard as the bus neared the center of town. As Gabe worked on the school forms, every so often a lurch of the bus would scare his pen into a crazy loop. He had to sign "Vernon Culligan" in a bunch of places: release for school field trips, permission to receive minor medical care at the school nurse's office, parent-teacher-student association, physical education liability release—Gabe didn't understand what some of it meant. Nevertheless, he dutifully wrote his

uncle's cramped signature. But what Gabe hadn't antici-
pated was all the contact information requested. Parent or
guardian. Doctor. Dentist. Emergency contact. Health in-
surance. All those phone numbers! Vernon didn't even believe in telephones!

"Nobody'd want to call me. And I don't want to talk to
no one. I'd as soon eat a weasel." It had not been Gabe
asking Vernon to get a phone, much as Gabe would have
liked to talk to his new friend Webber. No, it was the social
worker, Ms. Rodriguez. She patiently explained, despite
Vernon's red-faced cussing, the importance of the telephone. That owning a phone wasn't her rule. It was a state
rule. Child Protective Services required all residences,
foster or adoptive, to have a phone. Basic. Like food and a
separate bed for each child. Gabe liked the way she joked
with Uncle Vernon. "Mr. Culligan. I'm not asking you to
eat a weasel. In fact, I'd rather you didn't. All I'm asking
for is a telephone. I need to have a number for the forms.
I can't make you use the phone. You can let it sit there like
it came from outer space. But the bottom line is—you need
a phone."

"But—"

"Phone."

"Look, lady, I don't know where you come prancin' in
from—"

"Phone."

"You can't jus'—"

"If you want the boy."

Ms. Rodriguez won.

Vernon got the phone but never used it. He would

glare at it if it ever rang. Gabe was forbidden to touch it. The phone sat there, silent forever, eventually disconnected.

So Gabe struggled with his forms. Mrs. Pickering would be his emergency contact. *That's easy.* But what was her number? Should he ask Webber? No, that would get complicated. Pickering Pies! Yes, that was sure to be in the phone book. He would check at the public phone outside the school. The same for his doctor. But Gabe couldn't even remember his dentist's name. He had been there once, he knew. *Darn, what was that?* Gabe worked his tongue and tapped his pen. *Ah! Look at that!* An advertisement for a dentist, with a gleaming tooth and painted sparkle, glinted from an ad midway down the bus. Gabe copied the number onto his form. If only Uncle Vernon's old phone number would appear on a billboard.

In homeroom, Ms. Tsang flipped through the papers. "Your phone number's not written in. What's your number, Gable?" Gabe's silence led to the expected taunts and jeers. Janet was unusually quiet. She held her pencil poised, as if ready for dictation. Ms. Tsang finally said, "Is it the same as last year? I can fill it in for you from the paperwork from your elementary school."

"Yes," Gabe answered. "It's the same." He wished Guppy were at his feet right now. She wouldn't let kids hassle him, he was sure. She'd bark and snarl. Yeah, that would be the way. But then Gabe realized he hadn't heard her bark at all. Could she bark? Maybe she had a sore throat and he didn't know it. How do you take care of a dog's sore throat? He decided he would look in her mouth when he got home. Oh, if only school were done! He needed to check on Guppy!

At morning break, instead of meeting Webber, Gabe went to the school library and surrounded himself with reference books. *Breeds of Dogs. Care of Dogs. You and Your Puppy. Dog Training Made Easy.* Gabe tried to figure out what kind of dog Guppy was and how to cure a dog's sore throat. She looked like a German shepherd, tall, alert, ready, and lean. But her ears didn't perk up the same way and she lacked brown markings. Maybe a black Labrador, but larger, more wolflike. Gabe couldn't find exactly what breed she fit, and he couldn't find anything on sore throats, either, though he found lots on nuisance barking. *Well, maybe it's good she has a little sore throat.*

"Are you planning to get a dog, Gabe?"

Gabe shrank down in his seat and looked, open-mouthed and wide-eyed, at the tall figure of Mr. Boehm.

"I didn't mean to startle you." Mr. Boehm smiled and his goatee wriggled.

Though Gabe's mind raced, no words came to his lips. Instead, he lowered his gaze and fingered the edge of a page.

"Don't dog-ear the page," said Mr. Boehm.

When Gabe's hand sprang from the book and froze midair, Mr. Boehm gave a gentle laugh. "Just a little joke, Gabe, that's all. . . . You know, I like dogs too. I have a golden retriever. . . . I'll see you in class."

Gabe nodded, then studied Mr. Boehm's departing back. Gabe looked up "golden retriever" in the breeds book just before the bell brayed. A serene blond dog with folded ears like Guppy's stared patiently from the page. *What a nice friend for Guppy.* Gabe quickly reshelved the books and ran to class.

"I gave up on you for break," Webber said. "And I wanted to tell you my mom says fine. She wants you to meet us here, at the soccer field, at two o'clock. I have a game. Don't forget your stuff," Webber reminded him. Then he said, "Jeez, you stink."

Gabe didn't have a chance to respond, as Mr. Boehm greeted the class by introducing a poem by Robert Graves. Gabe sniffed himself—he had forgotten to take a shower all week. *Arrgh!* He missed the title of the poem but paid attention again as he heard students snicker. Mr. Boehm continued:

> *Children born of fairy stock*
> *Never need for shirt or frock,*
> *Never want for food or fire,*
> *Always get their heart's desire:*
> *Jingle pockets full of gold,*
> *Marry when they're seven years old.*
> *Every fairy child may keep*
> *Two strong ponies and ten sheep;*
> *All have houses, each his own,*
> *Built of brick or granite stone;*
> *They live on cherries, they run wild—*
> *I'd love to be a Fairy's child.*

The class had snorted and laughed at the marrying line, but Gabe noticed Mr. Boehm didn't mind. When he'd finished reading, Mr. Boehm asked the class to take out their writing assignments. "And how about you?" he asked the group. "What is your heart's desire? What do you want most in this world? A pocketful of gold? A pony? To run free and wild? How about you, Anneka? You were interested in this assignment."

Anneka ruffled the papers on her desk. She had written five densely filled pages. "I want there to be peace all over the world and no fighting and no more wars and people to stop wars and—" Mr. Boehm interrupted and asked her to read her first paragraph. She finished it in one long breath. Which was appropriate because the paragraph consisted of one sentence, one very long sentence. Mr. Boehm thanked her for sharing her work and asked Janet for her heart's desire. Janet, it appeared, had a very big heart, because she had many desires. She wanted to be president of the United States and also to preside over the United Nations. She wanted to win the Nobel Prize for mathematics and the same day accept an Academy Award for best actress. The list went on. And that was just the first paragraph. Mr. Boehm thanked her, too.

Joaquin, when asked, said he wanted to be the best athlete in the world. "Hey, that's not fair," interrupted Webber, "that's what I want. You cheated." His voice was sharp like bared claws.

The class held its breath, waiting for Webber to be dressed down. Joaquin had partly risen from his chair. Low *oohs* scuttled from several mouths and tensed the air.

"Joaquin, please be seated. Now, Webber. Let us

say that a delicious red apple sits here in the middle of the room."

Everyone stared at the chosen spot, empty of any fruit. Mr. Boehm continued. "And let us say that both you and Joaquin want that apple. Want it very, very badly. Would you say that he cheated to want the same apple?"

"No, but—"

"Okay, now, do you suppose that if you grab that apple, which both you and Joaquin so desperately want, the peace Anneka so desperately wants will be ruined?" Mr. Boehm continued after Webber grunted a "yeah." "And what do you suppose could have prevented the War of the Apple? Could all of Janet's power and glory, which she so desperately wants, have prevented the War of the Apple?"

The class agreed that Ruler of the World Janet could not have prevented such a war. And to Mr. Boehm's "What, then?" Joaquin offered, "Sharing it?"

"That's right, very good. Sharing it."

Webber said, "Aw, Joaquin, you can have it all, I'm sorry."

"No," replied Joaquin, "let's share it."

"No, I really want you to have it, 'cause I break out in weird red dots when I eat apples and my tongue hangs down like this and then I have ta flip it bach in my moufh. . . ."

During the laughter, Mr. Boehm said, "Excellent, I think I've heard everything I want to know about Webber's tongue. Now, back to the point. I want to hear from some-one who wrote about sharing. In essence, about love."

The room quieted instantly. Gabe turned as red as the imaginary apple.

"Ah. Gabe, I thought as much. Would you be so kind?"

But Gabe sat biting his lip and working his tongue. Mr. Boehm cut short a comment from Charley: "Ooh, Gabe loves Lucin—"

Then Janet spoke quietly and firmly. "I know I don't have all the power in the world. That was just a silly wish. But I would like to hear what Gabe has to say, and I promise no one will laugh at you, Gabe." She glared around the classroom.

Gabe furrowed his brow. Why was school so impossibly difficult for him? Why, when he tried so hard to blend in, did he stick out like a clown in a church? Why couldn't he just fade into the wall, thin out like paint, turn invisible? What was the quickest way out of this? He eased from his seat and walked toward Janet. He handed her his paper, then silently returned to his chair and looked out the window. Janet gave Mr. Boehm a questioning look.

"It's okay if she reads it for you, Gabe?"

Gabe nodded and Janet began.

"'What I Want Most in the World, by Gabe Pace.

"'When I think about what I want most in the world I feel selfish because it is not world peace or little kids never starving again. To want those things I think I would have to be a giant that could spin a little Earth marble in his big giant fist and tell the tiny people to stop fighting and share their food and other stuff. But I am not a giant and so what I want most in this world is not very big.'"

Janet stopped. No one else had been allowed to read more than the first paragraph. But Mr. Boehm asked her to please continue. She cleared her throat and read:

"'I want my uncle Vernon to know that I love him very much and that I'm sorry for all the trouble I caused. I want him to know that the tire swing we built makes me feel like I'm flying over miles and miles of countryside and the chestnut tree is always holding a pretty green umbrella over me. I want him to know that when I feel lonely I hear him talking in my head like he really is inside me. I want him to know that I will always be good and that way I won't ever have to go back to a foster home. I want Uncle Vernon to know that he is the best thing that ever happened to me.'"

Gabe sat staring fiercely out the window, his hand hiding his teary eyes. The class was silent. The bell rang its abrupt, skull-jarring clang. The students were asked to pass their papers forward. Webber tapped Gabe on the shoulder in his rush out: "See you at lunch, Gabe-man." When most of the class had departed, Mr. Boehm sat down in Webber's seat. Gabe had not moved, too afraid that if he did, he would crumble.

"I'm sorry, Gabe. I thought you wrote about a dog or other pet you'd want. I'm going to give you back your paper now. Maybe over the long weekend, you might find a way to read it to your uncle. Or leave it for him to read. I'm sure he'd be very pleased."

Mr. Boehm placed the paper on Gabe's desk and returned to the front of the class. Students from the next class dribbled into the room. Gabe wiped his nose on the back of his hand, gathered his belongings, and, without looking at Mr. Boehm, hurried from the room.

The rest of the school day passed relatively uneventfully for Gabe. No one mentioned his essay, and at lunch he lost, as usual, to Webber in a ball and foursquare-court game they had invented called Chicken Out. Finally the last class of the day arrived, but then the clock seemed to absolutely stop. Gabe was sure the minute hand had broken. *Come on, three o'clock.* Ms. Tsang's comments weren't helpful either.

"Why, Gable, what a strong use of perspective." Gabe had just drawn one diagonal line next to his lopsided tree for the topic "The Natural World." She tried again when Gabe didn't answer. "Gable, the shading technique there could be called chiaroscuro." The effect was the result of Gabe's pencil point's having snapped—he had tried to cover the smudge with more lines. Ms. Tsang finally shrugged and moved on.

At long last the three o'clock reprieve sounded and Gabe shot from the art room. He raced to the bus stop and caught the first bus just as it prepared to ease from the curb. Gabe tapped his feet together during the ride, then ran to Lapan Lane after he got off. But once again, he stopped, unsure and worried, at the mailbox. He cautiously opened the box and peered inside. He removed a letter addressed to his uncle from the Salem Veterans Affairs Medical Center. As he closed the rounded door, he spied another piece of paper in the box, stuck far inside. He reached his arm in and pulled out the paper. It was his letter to the Mystery

Card Writer, refolded in a different way. Gabe carefully unfolded it. There was no new message. But crossed out, again and again with heavy black strokes, was his postscript question: "Who are you?" Gabe, who had thought he knew the final reaches of fright, began to understand that there were lonelier and bleaker kinds of fear than he had imagined. He remembered the time he was hit, years before, by an older foster sibling when he had stumbled upon her and her boyfriend in the basement. "Those who pry, die," she had hissed. The harsh strokes of the card writer stung more than the girl's slap.

Gabe slowly walked to the house. *Please, Guppy, be home. Please be home.*

Yes! Guppy sat on Gabe's bed as she had the day before. "Guppy! Come here, girl!" She bounded toward him. He sat on the hallway floor as she licked away his tears. He tried to look past her loose black lips and surprisingly large fangs but couldn't get a glimpse of her throat. "Speak," he said to her. "Talk, bark. *Ruff.*" Though she was silent, she seemed fine. "That's okay, Guppy, you can be quiet. I'm quiet at school. That's okay." Guppy lay down and Gabe nuzzled his head on her stomach. He lay with her a long time, as if by his doing so, her fur and his hair, her body and his arms, would never be separated again.

Chapter 7

Besides bathing, Gabe had forgotten several other activities during the week. He had forgotten to lug the battered trash can and the bin of recyclables to the end of Lapan Lane for Wednesday trash pickup. He hadn't bought milk and bread as he usually did on Thursdays. He'd failed to buy a new packet of bus tokens from the driver. And he had not visited the bank to deposit Vernon's disability and Social Security checks, nor had he withdrawn cash for household expenses. Now it was Saturday and Gabe had decided that having your own house wasn't so great. He wasn't a fairy child and he didn't want to be. Although a pocketful of gold didn't sound too bad. Uncle Vernon kept a cash box in his upper left desk drawer. As Gabe dripped the few remaining splats of milk onto his morning cereal, he mused aloud about money.

Guppy was an extremely good listener, though she sometimes fell asleep or took a stretch. When she got up to rearrange herself in front of the refrigerator, Gabe exclaimed, "Yes, Guppy, good idea!" Gabe remembered the tally tacked to Mrs. Pickering's refrigerator. While Annie, Webber's little sister, and Gabe had watched *Cinderella* for the umpteenth time before the usual Saturday dinner, Webber had broken a living room lamp with a baseball. Mrs. Pickering had turned red with anger. It was the third lamp to fall victim to Webber's throwing arm. Gabe, no stranger to hitting and punching in several of his previous homes, had paled and trembled. But Mrs. Pickering had marched Webber to the crime scene and handed him a bag, broom, brush, and payback plan. "Clean it up, Cinderfella. You've struck out. I will deduct the lamp's cost from your allowance every week till we're square." Webber had moaned and grumped about the setback to his savings plan for the next video game. Every Saturday he would stare mournfully at the tally as if it showed the stats of a losing home team; then he would run off to play ball—outside.

At the top of a sheet of binder paper, Gabe wrote: Money Gabe Owes Uncle Vernon. Then he took his paper and tiptoed into the study. He eased open the drawer and took out the box. After removing money for bus tokens, he wrote the amount on his paper. It didn't look very official. Mrs. Pickering had always put the date on the tally. There, that was better. As Gabe replaced the box, now with the account sheet on top, he noticed a deep green envelope in the far end of the drawer. He pulled out the envelope and read:

To: Mr. V.R.C.

Oh, how Gabe wanted to open that envelope. The corners were bent; a tiny tear marred one edge and a coffee stain smeared the "C." The flap was tucked, not sealed, just like the cards to Gabe. He looked around. Who would know? Guppy, who sat by the desk chair? Guppy would never tell. Breathing rapidly, Gabe slid the flap open. But the moment he touched the slightly discolored cream-colored card inside, Guppy barked urgently. Gabe jumped and nearly ripped the envelope shoving the flap back in. He crammed the envelope, money box, and tally sheet into the drawer and slammed it shut. Guppy did not cease barking. She had run from the room and as Gabe followed, he tried to calm her. "Shhh, shhh, Guppy."

Guppy stood at the window in the front room, front paws on the sill. She bared her teeth; even her molars gleamed in the morning light. Her bark, thunderous and deep, reverberated from her throat like gunfire in an alley. Gabe looked through the window—the mailman, in his crisp blue uniform, peered at the house from inside his doorless white truck. His hand held the brim of his postal cap for a moment, his eyes narrowed; then he drove away. Unlike on weekdays, when the mail was usually delivered in the afternoon by a woman, on Saturday the mail was always delivered in the morning by a man.

Guppy barked and snarled, spitting white foam in her rage, for several minutes after the truck left. Gabe cooed at her, afraid at first to touch her. When she turned to him, her eyes were not only hard and piercing, but also wide with fright. More than fright, Gabe thought. Terror. Gabe continued to speak to her even though she didn't respond to his voice. "Guppy, please, it's okay. Down, Guppy, please. He's gone. He won't hurt you." At last, Guppy's growls softened and she pulled her paws from the sill. The fur along her back stuck straight up like porcupine quills, but she had quieted. She sat on Gabe's command and then lay down. Gabe caressed her and smoothed her fur. He murmured into her soft ears, and when she next looked at him, the fear and fierceness were gone from her eyes.

Gabe was exhausted, and Guppy panted as if she had just exercised heavily. Gabe led her to the kitchen and re-filled her bowl. He sat leadenly at the table and watched her slurp the water, then nibble at her back paw as if nothing had happened. When she nuzzled his leg, he startled from his daydream—he was still in his pajamas. He had to take a shower and get his stuff ready for the sleepover. The kitchen was muddy from Guppy's tracks, and he knew he should really do laundry. But that would all have to wait. Gabe wanted to be sure that he didn't stink at the Pickerings'.

A large shower stall with a sliding glass door nearly filled the tiny bathroom. To make his showering easier, Vernon had installed handlebars and a bench. Gabe liked to sit on the bench and let the water cascade over him like a tropical waterfall. But usually Vernon would grouse outside the bathroom: "Gabe, you using all the water this side of the Rockies! What in tramp stink are you doin' in there?" Gabe would sigh, pick up the soap, and call back through the door, "Just finishing up, Uncle Vernon." Gabe would hear his uncle continue to mutter as he stomped away.

Just as he missed his uncle's bedtime goodnights, Gabe found this first shower a lonely experience without his uncle's prodding. Even the water hitting the plastic bench sounded hollow and weary to Gabe. So when he heard a whine and a snuffle through the baseboard of the door, he slipped from the shower and let Guppy into the bathroom. She immediately licked the shower floor, stepping, as she licked, into the stall. Gabe, still dripping, followed her in, and thus began the ritual of the combined canine-human shower. He shampooed her and rinsed her and discovered that his chest, covered with clumps of her black fur, made him want to play ape. So he scratched under his armpits and grunted to her head-tilted gaze as he climbed, monkey fashion, onto the bench.

After the shower, with his towel wrapped around his waist, Gabe debated whether to pull Uncle Vernon's towel from the rack to dry Guppy. But the dog took matters into her own paws and gave a mighty water-flinging shake. Droplets coated every surface, including the mirror above the sink. Gabe quickly grabbed Vernon's towel, draped it over Guppy, and led her to the dog door. "You go out and play—go find a patch of sun and dry off." He shook out the towel. This was Guppy's towel now.

Gabe felt much better. He had survived another first

without his uncle. He had a new routine for his shower, and even if Guppy didn't always bathe with him, at least he knew she would wait impatiently outside the door.

Before Gabe left for the bus to take him to school, the soccer field, and the Pickerings', he checked the mailbox. A single letter for his uncle, with the oval window of another bill. Gabe added it to the short stack of mail at the corner of Vernon's desk. He knew he would need to deal, in some way, with that stack, but he didn't have time now. He looked around again. Guppy was still out back. He quickly opened the top left drawer, withdrew the green envelope, and pulled out the card. He read:

I have a secret.

Gabe wondered if somehow his card had spirited itself into Vernon's desk. But then he flipped it over.

You are the only one who truly knows.
RTO 23d INF DIV B/1-52d inf to GRREG

Gabe could not plumb the secret code. The puzzle made him feel the way train whistles did—making him think of faraway places and times. He replaced the note in the drawer and slowly walked to his backpack. He pulled out his English essay and a blank piece of paper. Sitting cross-legged in the hall, he wrote this cover note:

Dear Mystery Card Writer,
I am sorry I made you mad. I am sorry to

57

*leave Guppy for one night—I am giving her
extra food, like you said. I hope you do not
hate me. Here is something I wrote that Mr.
Boehm said I should let my uncle read. I wish
Uncle Vernon could read it.*

                                              Gabe

After another serious talk with Guppy about his whereabouts and planned return, Gabe gave her extra hugs. He filled several bowls with water and put out a large helping of food. He stuffed the money into his pants pocket, dumped his schoolbooks from his backpack, replaced them with a change of clothes, and left the house, stopping only briefly to place his note and essay in the empty mailbox.

The bus schedule was less regular on the weekend, and Gabe arrived after the start of the game. Webber played forward and had just scored the first goal. The Fullerton Furies, as the sixth-grade boys' soccer team was named, had a long, miserable history of losing. Coach Thompson looked with a misty-eyed smile at Webber, goalie Joaquin, and the rest of his new "men." Meanwhile, on the sidelines, Mrs. Pickering chatted with other moms, and four-year-old Annie played on the grass, making clover chains.

Gabe waved to Mrs. Pickering as he approached. She was a small woman—Webber was already taller than his mother—and her short black hair tufted out from her head. Her movements were quick and sharp, and when she came toward Gabe he thought she looked like a sparrow hopping and bobbing below a crown of wild feathers.

"Gabe, angel! Look at you. I think sixth grade agrees with you. You look as shiny as a new-minted nickel."

Gabe grinned. "Thanks."

"I started to worry your uncle Vernon might change his mind and not let you sleep over. Webber would have thrown a fit. But your uncle's not like that, is he?"

Mrs. Pickering and Gabe had a running conversation-nonconversation about Vernon. Usually Gabe deflected her questions about his uncle. But this time he spoke bluntly. "No, he's not likely to change his mind."

"Oh, a man of his word, then."

Gabe looked toward the field. "So what's the score?"

Mrs. Pickering smiled. "Oh, I don't know, honey. Annie! How are we doing?"

Annie had a unique yet precise scoring system for her brother's games. Yanking up another clover, she called, "One-oh. Eight, thirteen, three stop."

"You got that, Gabe?" asked Mrs. Pickering.

"I think so. We're winning one to nothing. Number eight—hey, cool, that's Webber—made the goal, number thirteen assisted. Then I think she means Joaquin stopped three attempts at goal."

But he was unable to ask Annie, as she abruptly stood, and, clutching her damp flowers, began running along the sidelines toward an approaching man and woman. Gabe had seen Webber and Annie's father a few times before. Mr. Pickering wore spectacles and a suit and had a potbelly. Gabe had not seen the woman before. She was young and her blond hair shone like new grillwork. Her spike heels sank into the uneven turf, causing her hips and red leather skirt to sway. Mr. Pickering put down his briefcase to pick up his daughter, then shook off the clover tiara she had plunked on his balding head. The woman held a lollipop at arm's length near Annie, who leaned way over and grabbed it.

"Lordy, look what the cat dragged in," said Mrs. Pickering. "Don't tell Webber I said that—our little secret, okay, angel?" Gabe nodded and she continued. "Well, I've got to go switch the pies anyway. I'll be back in a flash."

Gabe climbed up the nearly empty metal stands to the top row. He hugged his backpack and gazed at the green expanse of the field. He pictured Guppy jumping, chasing the ball, running between the surging players, her tail wagging high. He missed her terribly.

Beyond the end of the field, Gabe caught sight of a hearse slowly traveling along the road beyond the pine trees. His chest felt icy and he remembered the chill, stiff skin of his uncle on the floor. He squinted, trying to see better. He thought he saw the long snout of a dog hanging from the window of the passenger seat, but then the car passed beyond view. Gabe shook his head—now he was imagining Guppy everywhere.

Mixed with his thoughts of Guppy were his ongoing thoughts about the Mystery Card Writer. Gabe scolded himself for asking "Who are you?"—he knew better than that, especially after one unfortunate question he remembered asking his uncle.

"You ever kill anyone in the war, Uncle Vernon?"

Vernon had ground his teeth and sworn till his face splotched purple. Then he'd spat at Gabe: "Jus' how do you think I got to be sittin' here, snotrag talkin' to you, *boy*?"

Vernon had stormed off. He'd taken a long, solitary, wheezing walk beneath his trees, and on the way back, he had stopped to look up at the sky through the intertwining branches. As soon as Gabe had seen his uncle approach the back door, he'd hopped down from his perch on the kitchen counter, where he had been peeping out the window.

"You been waitin' all this time?" Vernon had asked Gabe, who was sitting with his hands folded at the kitchen table.

Gabe had nodded, worked his tongue in his cheek, and avoided eye contact.

"I don't never want you to pick up a gun, lessen you need to kill someone. My guns are off limits to you. And I mean that. You can mess around with your toy gun all you want. I don't care about that. But real guns are serious business, and you're too young. Lord knows, we was all too young." Vernon had stopped speaking; then he had added, "Come on, now, we've gotta fix the drainpipe afore the next rain. And you're the only one who can scramble up there. Come on and give old Vernon a hand."

Gabe stirred from his memories as a cheer rose from the home-team fans. Webber had just scored again, and after returning high fives from Joaquin and his team-mates, Webber looked at his father, who was checking his watch. Then Webber looked way up in the stands and waved to his best friend.

Chapter 8

Gabe and Webber had moved two twin mattresses onto Webber's bedroom floor. They jumped and tumbled on the mattresses as if they were on trampolines until Webber accidentally pushed Gabe toward the desk and Gabe's arm received a nasty slash from the corner of a drawer pull.

"Webber Andrew Pickering," Mrs. Pickering tut-tutted. "You simply cannot play that rough with Gabe. What will his uncle think when Gabe comes home after his first sleepover with a gash the size of the Mississippi running down his arm? Now, let's have a look at that."

She washed it while Gabe apologized for getting blood

on the towel. She shushed him and said, "Now, who cares about a towel? Not Holly Pickering. There, that's as patched up as I can get it. I'm going to read to Annie now. You okay?"

"Can I listen?"

"Of course you can, sugar."

Gabe listened to the storybooks with his arms wrapped around his knees. He was loving the sleepover even more than he had thought possible. He always enjoyed gazing at Mrs. Pickering's oversize bags and bins of flour, sugars, nuts, and spices. He liked running his fingers along the shelves stacked with mason jars of preserved cherries and apricots and peaches. But tonight, the after-dinner pie-making was like a party. Webber had turned on the radio and emceed a sing-along, clowning with a rolling pin. Everything seemed to glow; even the circles of pie dough and sprinkles of flour on the large black granite counter reminded Gabe of moons in a starry night.

But what really filled Gabe with the yellow and gold shine of contentment was the tuck-in after the stories. Mrs. Pickering pulled the covers snug around him, then kissed him on the cheek.

"You sleep tight, Gabe. I love ya, honey."

Gabe could feel his tears moisten the pillow. His throat knotted like a constrictor hitch.

After Mrs. Pickering had similarly tucked in Webber and warned him not to keep his friend up all night, she left to remove the final round of pies from the ovens. The boys immediately whacked each other with their pillows, the thumps mixing with whispers and giggles. Just as abruptly as Webber had started the tussle, he ended it.

"How old is Uncle Vernon?"

"Huh? Uh, I don't know."

" 'Cause I was just thinking that if your uncle Vernon got together with my mom, then we'd be brothers."

"Oh. . . . No, I don't think that would work."

"How come?"

"Your mom's too pretty."

"Is he ugly?"

"Well, he's never liked people to see him. I dunno. It just wouldn't work. Forget it, okay?"

"Okay, you don't have to get snooty. If you don't want to be brothers, fine. I wouldn't want to share my stuff with you anyway."

Webber had rolled away. After a pause, Gabe spoke.

"Webber?"

Webber grunted.

"Maybe we could pretend to be brothers."

"Nah, forget it, Gabe-man. Pretending's no good."

"Oh."

"Yeah. I can pretend all I want and my dad'll still never come back. Just stow it. I don't want to talk about it."

The boys were quiet, each thinking their own thoughts. Bellbottom stalked the hallway, and when Gabe quietly called to her, she proudly turned her head. She had no desire to associate with rangy boys lying on floor mattresses when she owned an entire king-size down pillow on Mrs. Pickering's bed. Gabe curled up again— Webber was already snoring in dreamland. When Webber flung out an arm and rolled onto his back, Gabe gently turned his friend back to his side.

Gabe closed his eyes tightly and, trying to sleep, thought of one of his uncle's bedtime homilies. "When you're in the chigger-bit dirt," said Uncle Vernon, "and they's strafing the jungle rot out of you, you can still be grateful it ain't raining buckets. And if it's raining buckets you can still be grateful they ain't snakes swimmin' by you. And if they's snakes swimmin' by you 'n' trying to swim up your pants, then you really are in a stinkhole and you have every right to say so and cuss out your grandmother's grave to boot."

The memory did help Gabe to sleep. But he dreamed a dream that was to haunt his nights for weeks to come; its chilling images even crept into his days. It began with a chaos of shapes and the frightening sound of someone being tracked through the woods. The tramp of boots, the crack of sticks, angry shouts, the whir-buzz of chainsaws, all swirling up from a mist. A mist that glowed white and sickish green. Trees crashed, making the ground shake and heave. Black claws of huge leafless branches lashed through the mist, then were swallowed by it until just one tree remained—huge and looming in the milky stir. A tire swing hung from a branch. Then the tire transformed into a figure covered by a billowing sheet, cinched at the neck, swinging below the tree . . .

Gabe cried out, "No, *no*. *No, don't!*" He lay on his back and clutched his throat as if being strangled.

"Sweetheart, Gabe, honey, wake up, it's okay, sweetie, wake up."

Mrs. Pickering soothed Gabe awake. His breaths choked out raggedly, and when he opened his eyes, his breathing became even harsher. They would find out, he thought in his half-waking state, find out and come for him. Then he would be punished. He thrashed, punched his arms wildly, and wrenched away from Mrs. Pickering. Only when he had pulled himself to a sitting position, hugging his knees and rocking on the mattress, did his breathing begin to calm.

Webber smushed his pillow over his ears, and Annie's small nightgowned figure stood in the doorway.

"You must have had a doozy of a bad dream. You okay, angel?" Mrs. Pickering asked. Gabe nodded, his head still tucked. She tried to pat his shoulder, but he jerked away. Annie started crying and Mrs. Pickering left to tend her daughter. By the time she returned to Webber's room, Gabe was curled on his side, pretending to sleep.

The next morning Gabe felt so guilty about disturbing everyone with his nightmare that he got dressed, straightened his bedclothes, and tiptoed downstairs with his backpack before the other children awoke. What could he do to make it up to Mrs. Pickering? Make her breakfast? Uncle Vernon would fix Gabe a special breakfast when Gabe was sick with fever and chills in bed.

"Can't make it to the mess hall? Well then, the canteen'll come to you." Gabe would be presented with a tall mug of warm, nasty-looking liquid with red and brown streaks. "Had to leave out the whiskey, but jig it, most of the rest is there. Go on, drink it down. Don't want to have to put it up the other end." Confronted with that image,

Gabe would drink the brew. Vernon would nod approvingly. "Yep, Bian Tam's secret recipe. Magic." And Gabe, after suppressing the initial urge to vomit, would indeed feel better. Whether it was because of the musky wet-leaf aroma of the cure or the handling of the ancient little bags of roots, dried fish entrails, and crushed herbs, sometimes Vernon would sit on Gabe's bed and talk about the war. "She kept a whole wall for an ancestor altar. Little kids'd be starving for somepin and there mama-san'd have three bowls of longans, mangoes, kumquat, chom chom, lychee, dragon fruit. Her eyes were black, pure black, and her nails were long and yellow. She was probably a hundred years old, but her skin was smooth as a *vu sua*. First time I met her, we were stuck on recon, far from the AO, deep in Indian country, the ops completely fugazi, the horn dead, and my RTO sick as skunkrot. She comes creeping by our ditch. '*Am duong* very bad,' she says. I follow her, carrying my RTO's sorry hide into her hut. She rubs him all over—eggs, coins, pinches his skin, tiger balm, what all. He comes round, makin' crazy talk 'bout bats and boll weevils, but at least he was alive." Then Vernon would look over at Gabe's wide eyes and laugh. "Yeah, Gabe, I think Bian Tam's done fixed you up as well."

Mrs. Pickering, dressed in a plum kimono-style bathrobe and scratching her spiky hair, entered the kitchen unnoticed by Gabe. "You feeling better this morning, sweetie?" she asked.

Gabe jumped from the kitchen chair and scrambled to catch it before it toppled.

"Yes, fine, Mrs. Pickering. I was just, I was just thinking about making breakfast for you, but then I didn't know what you liked."

"Well, that is simply the sweetest thing I have ever heard. You keep that up and you're gonna make some girl mighty happy. I'm giving you and your uncle a pie for the holiday." Mrs. Pickering flitted about the kitchen, flicking on her coffeemaker, slapping the orange juice container on the counter, and whisking milk into a bowl of pancake batter with her practiced hand. "Now, do you suppose your uncle Vernon would be interested in an exchange program?" she continued. "I've got one lazy bum of a sixth grader who I just might be willing to part with for a spell. I've a good mind to go in and ask your uncle when I drop you off this morning."

What! She can't come in! Now more than ever! Though Mrs. Pickering had always insisted that Gabe wave from the door when she returned him to his home on Saturday evenings, she had never actually met Vernon. Gabe turned as pale as uncooked dough.

"I'm sorry, sweetheart. Maybe I didn't explain," said Mrs. Pickering. "Webber and Annie's father is coming over to pick them up—they're even missing church. . . . And I'll be delivering these pies all day. Otherwise you could've stayed longer. You know that, don't you?"

Gabe recovered. "I can take the bus home," he said brightly. Fingering the packet of tokens jammed in his pocket that he had bought the day before from the driver, he added, "I don't want to trouble you."

Mrs. Pickering resumed her pancake preparation,

heating the syrup in the microwave and testing the griddle. "Oh, no trouble at all. We'll go when I take some deliveries for that part of town. Don't you worry about a thing."

Gabe felt he was becoming quite good at worrying. He bit his lip, which Mrs. Pickering took to be a sign of hunger. She piled a stack of four plate-size pancakes in front of him. Annie, rubbing her eyes and dragging a huge crocheted purple afghan, sat down at the table. "No syrup," she demanded.

"Well, good morning to you, too, sweetheart. Give Momma a kiss."

As Gabe and Annie worked their way through the pancakes, Mrs. Pickering left to wake up Webber. He finally appeared, tousled and grumpy, at the kitchen table.

"More syrup," he said.

By midmorning, Webber had revived, and he and Gabe played one-on-one at the driveway hoop. Webber's father's Mercedes rolled to the curb and the horn honked. Webber peered at the car, then ran into the house shouting, "Annie, he's here! And he's alone!" While Webber was inside, the horn honked again. Gabe looked around, then approached the car. The passenger window rolled down, emitting a breath of air-conditioned new-leather coolness.

"You're Gabriel, right?"

"Uh, no, sir. Gabe, for Gable."

"You need a ride home, Gable?"

"Um, I don't know. Mrs. Pickering was going to take me."

Gabe was instructed to tell "Mrs. Pickering" that she need not bother. Gabe found himself seated in the back of Mr. Pickering's car with Annie, a strawberry-rhubarb pie on his lap, while Webber ran his fingers along the coupe's dash, praising the features of various deluxe car makes and models. Gabe knew nothing of car styles. His uncle kept an aged, formerly beige Dodge pickup at the side of the property, and Gabe, though he had helped his uncle patch the engine with wire, electrical tape, and hoses, mostly believed the truck moved forward by virtue of his uncle's curses.

Gabe played hand games with Annie—rock, paper, scissors evolved to laser bomb, black hole, hurricane; and Gabe had trouble keeping up with Annie's ever-changing rules. Meanwhile, Gabe directed Mr. Pickering along the bus route, which was the only way Gabe knew, and was extremely relieved when Mr. Pickering made no objection to dropping him off at the end of the route. Gabe thanked him and stood waving, backpack and pie in hand, as Mr. Pickering drove off with his children.

When the car disappeared from view, Gabe walked homeward. He entered Lapan Lane, and with every step became more eager to see Guppy. Yet he hesitated at the mailbox. He looked up and could see Guppy's large head at the front room's window. He tugged at the stuck mailbox door till it opened with a twang. He grabbed the green envelope and ran into the house.

Chapter 9

If Gabe had had a tail, it would have wagged as excitedly as Guppy's at the reunion. They rolled and nuzzled on the hallway floor, then Gabe hugged-ran with her to the kitchen, where he filled her bowls. He sat with her on the kitchen floor as she steadily crunched the dry dog food. Gabe loved feeling her ribs as she ate; he even loved the water dribbling from her mouth after she lapped. She was perfect and she hadn't been taken from him. He could do this. Everything would work out okay.

Gabe opened his letter. He read:

I am not angry at you.

Gabe flipped the card. He realized he had been hold-ing his breath. He released it and took another.

You can call me Smitty.

Okay. That's good. Smitty. Thanks, Smitty! Once again, a tiny postscript followed:

P.S. Vernon knew you loved him.

Smitty, wonderful Smitty! Gabe looked again in the envelope to see if Smitty had returned the essay. He even rechecked the mailbox. But the essay was definitely gone.

Gabe opened the refrigerator and placed the pie on a shelf. Not much else kept the pie company. But with an entire Pickering deep-dish, lattice-topped pie and a belly full of pancakes, hunger would be a long time coming.

Gabe crawled through the dog door and called Guppy. Again they romped and ran, this time to the edge of Vernon's property. A ravine separated his land from a large area of undeveloped meadow and forest. In the distance looped the cloverleaf of the highway's on- and off-ramps. At night, from the top of the ravine you could see the headlights of cars and trucks traveling busily along the highway; few people used the exit—they favored those closer to downtown. But the highway was how Gabe had first been brought to Vernon's, and he liked it for that reason. In the car, Ms. Rodriguez had prepped him for meeting his uncle.

"He's gruff. Not used to kids. Don't let that worry you.

He's family, your mother's brother. That can make a difference."

Gabe didn't know much about his past. He only knew that his mother had died and most social workers winced when they mentioned her to him. He knew his father had never been part of his life. And he knew that since he'd been two years old he had lived in lots of foster homes in lots of states.

"Ms. Rodriguez?" he had said as her car curved along the exit ramp.

"Yes, Gabe."

"Can you, I mean, do you, well . . ." Even at nine years old, Gabe had understood that this was the perfect opportunity for him to learn what he'd always wanted to know. But he hadn't wanted to annoy Ms. Rodriguez.

"What, Gabe?"

"My mother," he had finally blurted. "Can you tell me about my mother?"

"Ah. She was just in the wrong place at the wrong time. That was a long time ago. Perhaps you can ask your uncle after you get to know him. We're almost there. This is his street. Lapan Lane."

Now, years later, Gabe still knew almost nothing about his mother. He stood on the lip of the ravine, Guppy at his side. How many times had he tried to ask Uncle Vernon about his mother? Surely, of all people, his mother's brother could lend Gabe a real memory of her, rather than the dim image of her long brown hair. Then one day, mere weeks ago, it had almost happened, right here, at the edge of the ravine.

"*Xin loi,* Gabe. I'm sorry," Vernon had said.

"Sorry 'bout what?"

"Sorry I near pickled my body. . . . Just like my dad, I s'pose. Your grandfather. My God, what that man wouldn't do for a drink."

Gabe and Vernon had been walking along the rough, loose-rock verge of the precipice. The sun had cast its long amber fingers against the darkening sky. The ground, spongy from a recent rain, had made Gabe sense the weight of each footfall.

Gabe had gathered his courage. "Did you know my mom?"

"No, Gabe, I didn't. I only met her once. You know, she 'n' I had diff'rent mothers, and she was quite a bit younger'n me. I was home, it was late sixty-seven, after two tours. Didn't know what to do wit' myself. My mom had already passed. I went to see my dad. I dunno what I expected. A pat on th' back. A toast at th' bar. Somepin, I dunno. He toasted me, all right. 'Lookee here at the fool,' he said to his buddies. 'Joined the army, not even drafted. Fighting a war so's rich folks ken send they's kids to National Guard duty. Army's full of stupid idiots.' Another fellow there bopped him one, and I just up and left. Two weeks later, wouldn't ya know, he kicks the bucket. Stroke. Just like that. I went to his funeral so's I could spit on his grave. But then there was this pretty little girl. Dark hair. Dark eyes. Solemn and quiet-like. You know, come to think of it, you remind me of her. Quiet, but real strong inside. Like you're made of tough wire— wire that might bend, but wouldn't never break. I signed

74

up again for the army—did ya know that? Yeah, the next day. To spite him, I guess. And 'cause I didn't think even a little girl'd show up at my funeral."

They had walked in silence. A nearby cricket had chirped mightily, and the sudden absence of his song when it stopped had made the quiet of the evening ring in Gabe's ears.

"I don't want you to die, Uncle Vernon."

"No? Why's that?"

" 'Cause, um, 'cause you're not like your dad."

Vernon had brought his palm up to the outer edge of his right eye. "Okay, Gabe. I'm tryin'. Please remember that. I'm tryin' the best I ken."

Gabe wasn't sure what Vernon had meant by that. The words had filled Gabe with a sadness as deeply blue and dark as the night sky. Was Vernon trying to love him? Gabe hadn't asked any more questions. He and Vernon had walked under the thick arms of the trees back to the house and in through the kitchen door. Vernon had flipped on his fan, then the bright white overhead light.

Soon after, Gabe had stood, pajama-clad, at the kitchen doorway. His uncle had sunk heavily into a kitchen chair.

"G'night, Uncle Vernon," Gabe had said.

"Goodnight, Gabe."

Gabe had waited for the usual scrubbed raw dash of wisdom, peppery warning, or juicy soldier's tale. Instead, Vernon had said, low and soft under the shirr of the fan, "I don't deserve you, Gabe. God in heaven knows, I don't deserve you."

Now, wrapped in his thoughts, Gabe walked along the edge of the ravine. He bent down and gave Guppy a long, hard embrace, sticking his face deep into her thick ruff of fur. "It's just you and me, Guppy. And we'll live off the fatta the land. Yeah, we can do it. Mrs. Pickering's pie and a big bag of dog food and the fatta the land. Huh, girl? You like that?"

Guppy's ears pricked and her body stiffened. Then, without a bark, she broke from Gabe's hold and shot diagonally down the side of the ravine. "Guppy, no, girl, you'll get stuck! We're not s'posed to play down there. There's poison ivy 'n' . . . What the—?"

Guppy had found a plank crossing the bottom of the crevasse, camouflaged by the same vines, creepers, and roots that formed the rest of the brambles far below. She easily ran up the other side and took off at full run. Gabe slipped down the embankment on his bottom, grabbing at roots and rocks, and reached the plank. He eased out on it, found it stable, then scrambled as best he could up the far side. For a second, he caught sight of Guppy running between two trees and headed in that direction, calling for her to return. He lost sight of her as she ran into a thicket. He stretched his neck and jumped several times, trying to see. But it was no use, and he blindly thrashed through thistle and kudzu. Then he stopped short. Was that . . . ? Yes, that really sounded like something heavy crackling over brush, the irregular thud of tires bumping a chassis on uneven ground, an engine gunning. Gabe looked toward the highway and tried to see the exit loop. But he was too low and the exit too far, and he really wasn't sure what he had heard.

Gabe desperately called Guppy. Over and over. And then there she was, loping easily toward him, her tongue lolling from the side of her mouth, her head tilted quizzically, almost comically, as if she wondered what game he wanted to play next or what trick he had up his sleeve. Gabe's arms were scratched and his gash had reopened, the bandage loose from the scramble. A few drops of blood fell to the mat of old leaves, and he held the bandage on with his other hand. Guppy sniffed his arm, then backed away and sat without a command. Gabe looked out toward the area she had come from, then sighed. "You're not to do that again, Gup. Someone might take you. Good dog like you, lots of folks'd want you. You stay close to the house, you hear?"

Guppy cocked her head. She accepted Gabe's rub behind her ears, then walked with him to the ravine. She looked once over her shoulder before she descended the slope. She waited on the opposite side. As he tripped and slid down the embankment, Gabe kept his eyes on her, as if, at any moment, between blinks of his eyes, she might disappear.

Once home, Gabe was too tired to bathe, or do the laundry, or attend to the ten other chores he thought he ought to do to catch up on the week. All he could manage was to refill Guppy's water bowl, then bend his head to drink straight from the kitchen spigot himself. He retaped his bandage using some Scotch tape that he wrapped around his arm; then he lay on his bed. Guppy jumped up with an easy leap and they both napped. Gabe slept unusually heavily, as motionless as a lost boat stuck in the humid afternoon.

After he awoke, he cut himself a generous slice of pie. As he ate, he talked to Guppy. Asked about her parents. Told her about the sleepover and about Bellbottom. He liked to run through Guppy's tricks, like rolling over and sitting up, and even though she failed on less conventional commands, like addition, he knew she was smart.

Gabe lay on the kitchen floor, rubbing Guppy's lower ribs, forcing her to twitch her back legs. Although he realized she must have been trained to wait in the house for his return, he worried about her recent escape. Maybe he and Guppy should run away together. They could find some hills to hide in—hills with caves and loose wood to make a fire. He could take one of Uncle Vernon's guns with him. "Guppy'd be a good hunting dog, huh, Gup?" Gabe could shoot a quail or a rabbit when they were hungry.

Nah. That's no good. Gabe remembered his little blue bunny. No, no shooting rabbits, no camping in caves, no fires. What could he do? He looked out across the black and white linoleum floor, the lines of the squares flaring away from him. Dirt and dog hair matted the floor. The fur of Guppy's ankles stuck out in muddy spikes. "Okay, Gup, let's start with you. Then we'll get this place 'clean as a cherry's kit.' That's what Uncle Vernon'd want."

Gabe had heard an awful lot about cherries from Vernon and had become respectful of them, despite their stupidity, impossible knuckleheadedness, and unfailing ability to "get picked off." He had wondered if he had been a cherry to Vernon—always new and making mistakes. Gabe had become sympathetic to the split and tender red fruit in a Mrs. Pickering's Honest Cherry Pie.

So Gabe and Guppy showered, then mopped, washed, laundered, and swept. Guppy was less talented, to be sure, at such matters. In fact, her shaking of wet fur and tramping through the kitchen after a visit outdoors tripled Gabe's work. And the repeated dropping of the tennis ball she had rescued from Gabe's toy shelf caused him to stop work for the ever-important game of fetch. Nonetheless, the house did, eventually, look more orderly.

Evening, with her blowing skirts of cooling breezes and rustling leaves, swirled her colors, first fiery, then deep blue, through the trees and around the house. Gabe fed Guppy, poured a bowl of dry cereal for himself, and sat on the floor eating the last of the flakes. He had already run out of bread, and he missed his usual sandwich. After Guppy had flexed her lean, muscled body, her large rib cage nearly touching the floor with the last stretch, and left for an after-dinner stroll, Gabe took a long swing on his tire. Returning from her walk, Guppy sat, head on her paws, and Gabe looked at her, then up at the new stars blinking between the rushing leaves. Vernon had liked gazing at the night sky too.

"You ever wonder if there's a heaven up there, Gabe?"

Streaks of light had marked the silent November sky as Gabe and his uncle lay on the back of the pickup, legs stretched out over the tailgate to watch the Leonid meteor shower almost a year before. Vernon had roused Gabe from his bed at two in the morning, and they had dragged blankets out to the truck. Gabe had been wrapped in the heavy plaid one. He'd wondered if that was why Vernon so frequently searched the sky—if he was trying to see heaven.

When Gabe didn't answer, Vernon had continued. "Sometimes I gotta believe there is. It can't all be for nuthin'—that's a cruel, sick joke."

"My momma's in heaven." Gabe had finally spoken. His quiet voice puffed small clouds in the chill.

Vernon had twisted to look at his nephew. "Yes, your momma's in heaven. I guess you do unnerstand after all, don'tchu."

Gabe had felt he understood less and less. He'd let the silence settle again. *Now's a good time,* he had thought. He had nearly gathered enough courage to ask about his mother's death when the loud, sharp backfire of a car on the night highway had cracked the air. In an instant, he had felt his blanket cocoon wrenched from the truckbed and he'd been tossed, still wrapped, under the back of the pickup. He'd smelled the cold rubber and tar of the tire and the oiled metal of the wheelbase as he had struggled from his blanket. He had never seen his uncle move so fast. Then the truck had shaken with the pounding of his uncle's fist, and Gabe could hear Vernon curse fiercely. By the time Gabe had managed to creep out from under the truck, his uncle had stomped off to the trees and the back reaches of his property. Gabe had shivered, retrieved the blanket, and curled up in the truck, as close to the cab as possible. He'd hugged his knees and waited. He'd no longer wanted to see the sky's celebration of white fireworks. His shoulder had been sore from where he had hit the ground, but he hadn't rubbed it. After half an hour, he'd heard his uncle return to the house, come back outside, and walk over to the truck. They had looked at each other in the dark.

"You okay?"

"Yes."

"Come on, then. Show's over."

Gabe had slid and crawled across the truck bed, and they had reentered the house. Gabe hadn't been sure whether to say goodnight again. After all, he had already wished his uncle goodnight when he had first gone to bed that night. Instead, he'd said, "I liked the shooting stars."

"Yeah? Didya make a wish on one?"

"Yes."

"Well, two fools, then. Me too. And I hope to God it comes true. Now, git on to bed, wouldya, and git some sleep."

And as Gabe had slept, the twinned wishes had spun through the frost night sky.

Chapter 10

Gabe paced the hall outside his uncle's study. A week had passed since he had come tripping home full of news of his first day at Fullerton Middle School, only to stop short inside the front door. He had barely stepped into the study for most of the week, and not at all since Saturday morning. Now here it was, almost evening on Labor Day, and Gabe had finally opened his schoolbooks to start and finish his holiday weekend homework, only to discover that he needed to enter the study.

In his rush to leave school Friday afternoon and return to Guppy, he had not read the paper Ms. Tsang had handed out at the end of art class. A permission slip. And a request for two dollars to cover student group admission to the Art Museum of Western Virginia in nearby Roanoke. A field trip for the entire sixth grade. Bag lunch required. First Friday in October. Check here if you can chaperone. Permission slips due now! The bottom of the paper held this postscript: "See Ms. Tsang if financial assistance needed."

Gabe chewed on this latest problem and explained it to Guppy. He concluded with: "There is no way I'm asking for 'financial assistance.' Can you imagine what Uncle Vernon would say to that? He'd blow a gasket. 'Don't you go beggin' for nuthin'! You ain't some street urchin beggin' for coins, and stealin' from they's other pocket while the idiot searches for a penny. No, you need somepin, you come and ask Uncle Vernon fair and square. You ain't never to steal or beg. You hear me?' "

Gabe was quite good at speechifying with Guppy as his audience. Guppy had ceased pacing with Gabe midway through the lecture. She lay stretched like a sphinx, her head erect and her eyes on Gabe. When Gabe finally asked her to come, his talking done, she promptly rose and they entered the room together.

Gabe eased open the money drawer and removed not only two dollars for the field trip, but also money for groceries. He worked his tongue inside his cheek as he updated the money tally. He looked once at Guppy and decided not to risk another peek into the dark green envelope, which lay so temptingly close to the money box. He placed the permission slip on the desk and used a black pen to sign his uncle's name. Vernon kept his pens in a wooden holder Gabe had made—the result of a lesson on power drills. They had drilled five holes in one end of a five-inch section of a two-by-four. Vernon had tossed it into the scrap heap, lesson done. But two weeks later, when Vernon was out on a walk, Gabe had retrieved the wood, sanded it, then dimpled the words "For Uncle Vernon" on one wide face with a nail. Vernon had surprised Gabe on the final stroke of the last "n" so there was a flare off to one side of that small hole.

"Whatchu doin' there, boy?" Vernon had demanded.

"I, um, I dunno."

"Sure you do. I don't tolerate lying. Don't test me. Whatchu got behind your back?"

"It's a present," Gabe had said miserably. "Here."

Vernon, frowning, had turned the block over and over. "What's it for?" he'd asked.

"Christmas."

Vernon had paused at this response. "But it ain't even Thanksgiving yet."

Gabe hadn't responded, but had blushed instead.

"Okay, Gabe, I'll tell you what. Since I got to see my Christmas present early, I'll let you get a glimpse of yours. But only a glimpse, now. And you got to promise you won't go poking around keeping track of it. And I won't go fishin' for my present—I know you didn't finish it—it ain't even signed."

Vernon had handed the block back and turned to a far corner of the shed.

"Okay, ready? Only a peek."

Vernon had whipped back the corner of a tarp as Gabe

stood leaning to one side to get as good a look as possible. All he'd seen was a pile of wood. When Vernon had turned back, he had laughed to see Gabe's puzzled look.

"Okay, Gabe, that's it. I hope you'll like it as much as I know I'll like mine."

Gabe had blushed again, then popped the block under his shirt so Vernon couldn't see it anymore. And on the morning of their first Christmas together, Gabe had woken up to find the same tarp covering a bulky rectangle in the tiny front room. Gabe had grinned and let out a gasp, because sitting atop the tarp was a little Christmas tree with three miniature wooden ornaments hanging from its few branches. He hadn't thought they'd have a tree. Gabe had raced by his uncle and returned from his room with a wrapped present. He'd carefully placed it under the tree. Vernon had unwrapped his present and started to scratch his chin, but then smiled when he found a Halloween pencil from Gabe's fourth-grade class party tucked inside the wrapping. Gabe had removed the tarp and found a new student desk, hand-built by Vernon to replace the plank and sawhorses that Gabe had been using.

Gabe put his uncle's pen back in the wooden holder, then swiveled the block to look at his signature. At the bottom right-hand corner he had tapped out "Gabe" in small letters with the nail. Looking at it now, he could see that the area over his name was discolored and rubbed marble-smooth. He felt a chill, almost as if his uncle had reached out with his rough thumb and touched Gabe himself.

Needing a paper clip to attach the money to the forged permission slip, Gabe slid open the slender drawer just below the lip of the desktop. He found not only a paper clip, but also three other items of interest. One was a checkbook; the other two were square white envelopes addressed to Mr. Vernon Culligan and Gabe in a familiar flowing, looped script. Gabe peered at the return address—*yes!* Two letters from Mrs. Pickering. *Wow!* And his name was clearly on both! Gabe opened both envelopes and discovered two Christmas cards, each with a manger scene on the front; one had gold halos, the other a blazing silver star. Inside the silver card Mrs. Pickering had written, "Merry Christmas and may the Lord's Blessing be upon you. From Holly, Webber, and Annie Pickering." When Gabe opened the second card, a photograph fell out. Webber and Gabe grinned and waved from the pool, their hair shiny wet. Gabe remembered when Mrs. Pickering had taken the picture—the end of summer before fifth grade. By then Gabe had been completely comfortable in the water, and the boys were especially happy to be together, as Webber and Annie had just returned from a two-week trip with their father. Gabe read the added note: "Merry Christmas and May God Bless You. What a joy your young man is. We love his visits. Here are two pictures you might enjoy. Please feel free to give me a call anytime. We would love to have Gabe sleep over once you feel he is ready. Happy Holidays! Holly, Webber, and Annie." Mrs. Pickering had written her phone number below the names. Gabe searched both envelopes, then the drawer, yet could not find another photo. But balled up in a far corner of the drawer was a piece of paper.

Gabe carefully opened the crushed paper. His uncle's handwriting was even more crabbed than usual, and many areas were blotted out. Gabe held the paper close and read:

> *Dear Mrs. Pickering,*
>
> *Thank you for your cards. Thank you for taking in Gabe and feeding him and fussing over him. Thank you for the pies you give him. They sure is the best pies I ever had. I don't rite letters much but to one poor fellow so I'm no good at it. I tried riting this letter many time. Thank you for inviting Gabe to sleep over. Gabe is more than ready. I know that. But I need to see him safe and sound in bed every nite. Most likely this is hard to figure. But heres the real reason for this letter. I need to ask a big queston of you. Gabe can't know.*

Around the last two sentences were large areas crossed out, and, try as he might, Gabe could not make out any more words. He examined the date on the letter and breathed in sharply. It was dated exactly one week ago. The same day he had started sixth grade. The day Vernon died. Gabe began to weep. He took the paper and joined Guppy, who lay squeezed under the desk. Gabe wrapped his arms tightly around her neck and coiled himself into as small a curl as possible. He rocked a long time with her, his face buried in her coat. Then he

took a pencil from the wooden holder and wrote this
message:

> Dear Smitty,
>   I was thinking maybe you miss Guppy
> and maybe we could all live together, you,
> me, and Guppy.
>
> Gabe

Chapter 11

After reading the spelling list aloud, Mr. Boehm explained, "Today we begin our first book of the year. Usually we read this together in the winter. But because of your field trip to Roanoke next month and the exhibit on art and nature, including, I'm told, the Arctic, it's more appropriate to read it now. Before we start, who would like to guess why the book is titled *The Call of the Wild*?"

Webber immediately climbed on top of his seat, pounded his chest, and roared a mighty Tarzan call. The kids hooted loudly; Gabe was surprised by Mr. Boehm's calm reaction to the noise.

"Very good, Webber. Now please come up to the front of the room."

The class sniggered and clucked as Webber climbed down from his chair.

"I was just kiddin'," he whined.

"You're not in trouble, Webber."

Webber brightened. "No?"

"No. In fact, I'd like everyone to stand next to their chairs. Come on, everyone up." After the scraping of chairs, Mr. Boehm continued. "Whether you realize it or not, the story of Tarzan is about the animal, wild side that we harbor within. In essence, when we make monkey sounds or pound our chests, we hear the call of the wild, the 'victory cry of the bull-ape'—our primate relatives. What does 'primate' mean? . . . Lucinda."

"Monkeys and stuff. Like apes."

"Yes, those are primates. Extra-credit homework for tomorrow: write down a definition of 'primate.' Okay, Webber and class, when I say go, you all have thirty seconds to heed the call of the wild. Here are the rules: you may not climb on or touch anything, you may not touch each other, but you are free to move around the room and let out your inner primate. When I say stop, you must freeze, in whatever position you're in. Questions? Ready, go!"

The children scratched their armpits, snorted and howled, monkey-danced, bobbed and twirled, gaped curiously at Mr. Boehm as if he were an alien, and generally caused a ruckus. When Mr. Boehm yelled, "Three, two, one, freeze!" everyone froze, each trying to have the most outrageous position and expression at the end. Each, that is, except Gabe. He had stood when told, and had even halfheartedly made a few soft monkey noises, but he had stayed by his chair and gazed out the window at the "freeze" call.

Mr. Boehm looked over the class, and his gaze stopped at Gabe. "Very good. You are all excellent at monkeyshines. You can unfreeze now, and as a special reward for leading us in this exercise, Webber gets an extra assignment. He can pick one student to help him with this homework, due tomorrow. He needs to bring in the name of the original Tarzan book, the author's name, and the year it was published."

Webber groaned but returned to his chair. He immediately asked Gabe to help him. Gabe shrugged, then turned to listen to Charley, who had been chosen to begin the reading.

Soon the bell rang and the students instantly gathered their belongings and charged out of the room. Except for Gabe. He sat, holding the book on his lap behind his backpack.

"Gabe, are you okay?"

"Yes, sir. Sorry. Fine," Gabe mumbled as he stood. He had barely made it to school that morning. He couldn't stop thinking about the letter, about his uncle struggling to write just before it happened. And he had been writing about Gabe. It was all too much. What did it really matter anymore? They could go ahead and send him to a foster home. Send him to jail, for all he cared. Except he would miss Guppy. A big except. He had to keep up a show.

"Are you worried about your grade?"

Gabe looked down at the "C" written on his spelling quiz. "I forgot to study."

"Do you think you can study this week?"

"Yes, sir."

The next class of students began to spill into the classroom. Mr. Boehm said quickly, "Okay, I'll let you go. But Gabe, could you do me a favor?"

"Yes, sir."

"Could you not call me sir?"

This request caused Gabe to smile a little. He nodded at Mr. Boehm, and when he left English class, his feelings of loneliness eased ever so slightly.

In math, though, Gabe had to suffer Janet's twitchiness next to him for the bulk of the quiz time, as she had turned her paper in early. Time was called before he had finished, and Mrs. Garvey, with her severe gray-streaked bun, scolded him for putting his pencil down too slowly. She also called him to the board to work a problem on decimals and he guessed wrong on the number of zeros. Mrs. Garvey, fond of rapping the board with a pointer stick, made Gabe say aloud with her, "One one-hundred-thousandth has a decimal, then one"—*rap*—"two"—*rap*—"three"—*rap*—"four"—*rap*—"zeros, then a one." He had jumped with each rap. As he slinked to his chair, she turned to the class.

"How many zeros if you write the same number as a fraction?" she asked crisply.

Janet's hand shot up. "Five zeros in the denominator," she replied when called on.

"Very good. Now that it's all clear, let's move on."

Clear as mud. Four zeros the same as five zeros? Now, that didn't make sense at all. It was worse than a hundred percent being one. There were so many rules in math. Maybe that was why Gabe was no good at it. He was breaking so many other rules that he couldn't keep the math rules straight.

Gabe jerked up in his seat as Mrs. Garvey gave the next problem—it was as if she'd read his mind!

"Now for a word problem. Four criminals decide to rob a bank. They steal one hundred thousand dollars. They divide the money equally. As soon as they do that, they are caught by the police and put in jail—for a very long time." Gabe thought she would set her piercing gaze on him, but instead, she swept it over the whole room. Then she finished, "What percent of the money did each criminal take, and how much money is that?"

Gabe thought so much about the police part of the problem that he had trouble figuring out the answer.

He sighed and doodled a picture of Guppy on his workbook.

"That your dog?"

Class was over and again Gabe had dawdled. Janet stood over him pointing at his drawing. Gabe slammed his workbook closed.

"No," he said, then winced.

"I have a horse, you know. His name is Espresso."

"Oh. A boy horse."

"Yeah, well, he's a gelding."

At Gabe's blank expression, Janet laughed. "You don't know what that is, do you?"

Gabe shook his head and looked at the door.

"His nuts were cut off." She made a snipping motion in the air. Now Gabe really winced.

"I gotta go," he muttered, edging away. He ran from the room.

Outside he caught up with Webber, who had already wolfed down half his lunch. Mrs. Pickering packed big lunches. Gabe had been so sluggish that morning that he hadn't had time for breakfast and had only wrapped a piece of pie for lunch. Like donuts, pie wedges didn't do well in backpacks. He gingerly unwrapped an edge and started eating.

"Yesterday I had the most boring day ever," complained Webber. "Grandma's house. You have to say things five times. Then she still doesn't remember and you go through the whole thing again. Then she called me Terrence. Terrence! That's my uncle's name—my mom's brother. You know, the one we visited last Christmas in California. Now, that was fun. Disneyland, Universal Studios, the beach. He's got lots of friends. And you don't have to repeat yourself seventeen hundred times."

Gabe enjoyed listening to Webber. It was comforting to hear his voice, to watch his sweeping gestures, to follow the wide range of his emotions. Was this how Guppy felt with Gabe? Was this how Lennie felt with George?

Gabe looked away as Joaquin, spinning a soccer ball, approached the duo.

"Wanna play? We could set up a goal over there and you could practice shots on me."

"Sure!" Webber was up in an instant. He grabbed the

ball and dribbled it toward the grass. At the edge of the table area, he turned and yelled to Gabe. "You can come too."

"Nah, that's okay." Gabe waved his pie crust in the air.

Webber shrugged and ran off with Joaquin. Gabe's shoulders sagged as he started to worry about the note he had left in the mailbox that morning.

Maybe Smitty would cross everything out, or rip his note to shreds. Gabe didn't want to think about it. He glanced around and saw Janet looking in his direction. She quickly turned aside and chatted to Brooke. Gabe grabbed his backpack and left the lunch area.

In the library, he slipped into a chair in front of a battered computer terminal. Even young Annie was better than Gabe on the computer, but he eventually found information on *Tarzan of the Apes*. He was surprised the library didn't own the book. So he read about it. Hmm. He didn't know that Tarzan had taught himself to read—that wasn't in the Disney movie. Tarzan had grown up without parents and turned out fine. More than fine. He was a hero, and brave. And strong.

The bell rang and the rest of the day passed without incident. Gabe walked four blocks to the supermarket, bought milk, sandwich supplies, and Honey Smacks, then caught the bus at the closest stop. By the time he reached the mailbox, he was tired and his grocery bag dragged on the ground. He removed the deep green envelope, then peered into the box. At least his own note wasn't there. When he saw Guppy's large head in the front window, her breath misting the glass, his energy returned and he ran in for the usual roll on the floor.

Sitting on the hallway floor, his legs draped over Guppy's side, Gabe opened the envelope and removed the cream card.

I cannot. Do not ask again.

On the flip side:

Time does not heal, but may allow us opportunities to learn.
Let us honor Vernon's memory.

Smitty was confusing, but at least he wasn't angry. Gabe was sure that Smitty was the "poor fellow" mentioned in Uncle Vernon's letter to Mrs. Pickering. Maybe Smitty had no money at all and didn't want to be beholden. That would be just like a friend of Vernon's. The thought of Uncle Vernon's having a friend was so warming to Gabe that he smiled.

Gabe led Guppy to his bedroom and cleared out the top left-hand drawer of his desk. Extra binder paper, a few knickknacks from various class parties, a pink eraser, and a broken pencil were easily moved to other drawers. Into this special drawer Gabe put Smitty's cards, the fan button, the blue bunny, and the letter from Uncle Vernon. Then Gabe closed and opened the drawer several times. Sometimes he would touch an item or read one of the cards. Finally he closed the drawer and ran his hand over the sanded, shellacked surface of his Christmas-gift desk.

Gabe fed Guppy, then fixed himself two peanut butter

and honey sandwiches. When Guppy left for her usual after-meal stroll, Gabe cautiously approached the study. Determined to find everything he possibly could, he searched every drawer of Vernon's desk.

Not much rewarded his efforts. There were bank records and some bills. The first copy of the school forms. A bundle of drawings and scrawled pencil writings by Gabe, including a test with a "100% Excellent work!" in red across the top of the paper. In a bottom drawer, however, lay a locked file box. "Built to withstand fire and natural disaster" was printed on the label. Gabe at first tapped the box, then tried to open the lock, then shook and outright banged the whole thing.

Just as he was ready to try to smash the box against a corner of the desk, he heard someone knock on the front door. A woman's voice cut through, aimed like a spear at Gabe's chest.

"Mr. Culligan! You in there? Vernon Culligan!"

Gabe's thoughts ran helter-skelter. Should he hide? Vernon never locked a door—the woman could just walk in. He could pretend to be Vernon and yell at her. But what if it was the police?

"Good dog, now be a good dog. Mr. Culligan! Gabe!"

When Gabe heard a low growl, he sprang to the door and whipped it open. This was no time for Guppy to go nuts. Ms. Rodriguez stood on the step, her eyes not leaving the dog. Guppy's lips curled so that her fangs shone in the dusk. When Gabe called Guppy, she obediently brushed through the door and sat next to him, her gaze once again fixed on the intruder.

"Well, Gabe, good to see you. You remember me?"

"Yessum."

Ms. Rodriguez shifted her weight. She was a trim woman with an easy smile, elf-bright eyes, and a brief-case, which she placed on the stoop. She held out her hand and Gabe reluctantly shook it.

"That's a fine-looking dog. I have to admit, he scared me."

Gabe's tongue worked furiously in his cheek, and he felt unable to look at Ms. Rodriguez. His world was rapidly collapsing.

"She's a good dog," he said.

"Right. . . . Well, is your uncle at home?"

Gabe didn't say anything, and Ms. Rodriguez broke the silence with a little laugh.

"Gabe, I'm not here to take you away, if that's the thought scurrying around behind that worried look of yours. You know your uncle adopted you fair and square. All done. No more foster homes. You understand that, right? He explained all that to you, right?"

"I, uh, I wasn't sure."

"Hmm. Look, can I come in? If he told you never to let anyone in, that's fine, I'll just come back tomorrow when he's here."

"You can come in. You don't need to come back no more."

Ms. Rodriguez laughed again. "Hospitality must run in the family." Then she added, "You expect him soon?"

"Maybe," he said as she walked by him. He didn't like

the way she looked around, as if she could see straight through walls. She turned to him.

"I noticed his truck was here."

"Yeah, he's out for a walk."

"I see. Can we sit down?"

"Sure. . . . Why not?" No visitors came to the house; it had been a long time since Ms. Rodriguez had last been there. Gabe tried to think of what Mrs. Pickering would do. "How about the kitchen?" he said.

Ms. Rodriguez nodded her head and followed him back. When Gabe offered her the last slice of pie and some milk, she agreed. She sniffed the milk before she took a sip.

"So, your uncle likes to walk by himself?" she asked.

Gabe considered her question. Why had she come here? She was clearly asking something more. He had to get rid of her suspicions.

"Sometimes. Lots of times we walk together, with Guppy, of course. But I had to study."

"I see."

"Yeah, Uncle Vernon makes sure I study. He doesn't want me to be a dope."

"Oh? Does he call you a dope?"

"No way. He says he's a dope, but I don't think so. He teaches me loads. See that dog door? I put that in."

"Nice work. Hmm—good pie, too."

"Thanks. Mrs. Pickering made it. Well, I helped a little."

"Mrs. Pickering?"

"Yeah, Webber—my best friend's mother." Would Ms. Rodriguez ever leave?

Ms. Rodriguez looked around the kitchen and at Guppy. "Did I ever tell you how I found your uncle?" she asked.

"No, ma'am." Now, finally, something interesting. Gabe leaned forward in his chair.

"Actually, it was rather easy. When your mother was four, her father died. Your grandfather. Funeral records are very handy for social work, as full names and other identification are used. That's when I discovered your uncle's name. Then it turned out his name was all over the government computer system from his years in the service. He's a highly decorated soldier, you know. Did he ever tell you about his medals?"

"He got medals?"

"I figured as much. Good old Vernon. He's not so old, though. Just gives that appearance. Took him a long time, I think, to sort it all out."

Gabe stared wide-eyed at her. "Gee, I'd like to see his medals."

"Why don't you ask him?"

Gabe squirmed. "I don't think so."

Ms. Rodriguez looked closely at Gabe.

"Why?"

"He's, um . . ." Then Gabe looked directly at Ms. Rodriguez. "He don't like prying."

Ms. Rodriguez smiled. "No, I suppose he doesn't. And I don't suppose you do either. Well, I guess I'll be on my way. I'm sorry I missed Vernon. Things have been hectic with my upcoming transfer to Richmond, and I don't think I can make it back here."

"Okay."

"And you should study."

"Yes."

Gabe cleared her dishes and she picked up her brief-case. They walked together, with Guppy, to the front door. Suddenly she turned to Gabe.

"He's not really out for a walk, is he?"

Gabe didn't answer, but instead dug his fingers deeper into Guppy's flank.

"He's the one who . . . ," she began. "Well, anyway, I think he doesn't want to see me."

"No, it's not that, it's just . . ."

"That's okay, Gabe. I understand. He values his privacy."

She picked up her briefcase. Gabe looked at the floor.

"Goodnight, Gabe."

Gabe perked up. "G'night, Ms. Rodriguez."

He closed the door before she cleared the front step. Gabe gave an unnecessary "Shhh" to Guppy behind the front door and crept to the front window. As he peered out, he saw her look toward the mailbox. Then he watched her put a manila envelope in the mailbox and finally drive away.

Chapter 12

Sitting on his bed with Guppy, Gabe opened the manila envelope. Inside was a letter typed on county government stationery.

> Dear Mr. Culligan:
>   I received your note requesting information about Gabe's mother. As you know, not much is known about her life. I trust you will be as gentle as possible in sharing these reports with him.

Since I am transferring to the Richmond
office, I regret that I cannot follow up further.
Please feel free to contact the local office with
any future needs.

It has been a true pleasure to work with
you. My regards to Gabe.

Sincerely,
Maria Rodriguez, MSW

Behind the letter was a packet of papers, including copies of newspaper articles. The headlines read: "Unknown Woman's Body Found," "Toddler Left in Car—Police Seek Info," and "Murder Victim in South Dakota Linked to Montana Orphan." The articles told of a violent end to his mother's life. She had been taken from a parking lot as she walked to the car that she and her son lived in. Her two-year-old son had been left to sleep in the car while she was driven in a white van across the state line. She had been murdered, and since no papers were ever found near her or in her unregistered car, it took the police some time to identify the boy. According to the police record, the criminal was eventually caught and convicted of several murders.

The only item in the envelope that was about Gabe's mother's life rather than her death was a grainy copy of her high school graduation picture. The photograph trembled in Gabe's hands, as if his mother also shook with delight to see her beloved once more. Her eyes, as Vernon had said, were large and dark like Gabe's.

Gabe looked into Guppy's almond-brown eyes, then

felt the wet rush of her breath across his back as he clutched her.

Gabe missed another Wednesday of school.

It rained all day, a heavy, humid rain that thickened the air between the drops. Gabe spent most of the day curled up in bed. Sometimes he plucked little tufts from the plaid blanket. It was in this numb mood that he wandered into the study that evening and paid the electric and other bills.

The next day, Thursday, he again went to school. In English class he gave the correct answers about Tarzan's author, but didn't feel any better after doing so. Then he secretly read the end of *The Call of the Wild* while another child droned aloud through Buck's first encounter with snow, Buck tasting the melting snow as if it were liquid shame. Gabe read because he needed to know whether Buck survived. Not only because he could so easily picture Guppy living free and wild, her great ribbed chest heaving after a run, and not only because if Buck died it would mean the death of so much more. Gabe read because he needed to know a story could end.

As September wore on, Gabe's quiet ways allowed him to glide through pretty much unnoticed in most of his classes. Except for English. In Mr. Boehm's class, he became known and admired as the kid with the answers. Mr. Boehm rarely called on him, but when he did, the class stopped twitching and turned to face Gabe. Mr. Boehm asked Gabe the toughest questions, the ones the rest of the kids secretly thanked their lucky stars they did not get asked. Questions like "Why does Jack London call life a 'puppet thing' on page twenty-four?" And Gabe, commanding attention with a quiet pause, would answer, "Because Buck didn't decide he wanted to go to Alaska. He was stolen and taken there. And that's what happens in life. You don't control it. Things happen. Maybe things you wished would never ever happen. Or maybe things you didn't ever think about 'cause you'd never even think they was possible." Mr. Boehm would look at Gabe, stroke his goatee, and say, "That's right. Very good. And Buck knew, instinctively knew, that with the twists and turns of fate, he would have to adapt or he would die."

Indian summer passed; the leaves darkened, then began to color. Gabe enjoyed several Saturday night sleepovers and helped Mrs. Pickering with the now endless orders for apple pie. He always looked forward to the tuck-in and cheek kiss, but he barely slept for fear of another nightmare. At the soccer game on the last Saturday in September, Webber told him the sleepover was canceled—Webber's grandmother was too sick. Webber's kicks during the game were so hard and wild that another player almost got hurt.

Throughout the month, Gabe's mailbox friend, Smitty, continued to leave and receive notes. Sometimes he would tuck an old note from Vernon behind the new cream card for Gabe.

> Smitty
>   You get youself a dog. That's what you
> need. I'm done with dogs but that don't mean
> they ain't worth the trouble.
>   Sniffer

Or a more recent one:

>Smitty
>We put blocks on the pedels and Gabe
>near broke my back driving the truck. But we
>had a ~~lauf laf~~ But we had a good time. He
>still loves them honey and peanut butter
>sanwiches.
>>Sniffer

These notes were crammed on the same cards that Smitty had left for Vernon. Gabe liked the differences between Smitty's and his uncle's writing. It made their friendship alive, like a conversation. The dog recommendation was written around Smitty's brief comment:

>The days are long; nights, longer.

The truck note was on the same card as:

>I had to do a pick up again. Guppy is a
>good driving companion, as long as the
>authorities are avoided.

Gabe, however, liked Smitty's cards too much to send them back, and continued to use his loose-leaf paper to write his letters, even though Smitty left plenty of room on his cards. When Gabe wrote to Smitty asking about Vernon's name, Sniffer, Smitty's response was short:

Everyone had a nickname.

Another time Gabe told Smitty about his dreams, the noose and hanging ghost under the chestnut tree. After a long description, Gabe wrote:

> *When I close my eyes, I see bad things, so*
> *I try to keep my eyes open a lot. Sometimes*
> *Guppy runs in her sleep but I think she is*
> *running to chase a ball or just because she*
> *likes to run. Sometimes I wish I was Guppy.*
> *Gabe*

Smitty's return note was one of his longest.

> *It's okay to dream or have terrible thoughts.*
> *It doesn't mean they will come true, or that*
> *   you are wicked.*
> *Dreams are a gift and a curse.*
> *Wishes make us human.*

Gabe was so comforted by the note that he did not suffer the same nightmare for a whole week. He kept all the cards in his special drawer. He also added his mother's picture, but the rest of the manila envelope sat in the bottom drawer of Vernon's desk, on top of the locked fire box. Gabe had decided he didn't need to know more secrets and never fiddled with the box again.

Guppy, however, remained a never-ending source of interest to Gabe. He studied her every motion, imitating her head tilt and eyebrow lift, or her total-body stretch and shudder, her back feet together like a ballerina's. He found the downiest fur just behind her ears that he liked to rub with his lips, then *pfuft* with a little blow that made her shake her head. She accepted all his yammerings and pettings and in return she nuzzled him with snuffles and pretend nips. They slept, bathed, and ate together. Gabe would take long Saturday-morning walks with her, as her behavior after the postman arrived the second Saturday was, if anything, more terrifying than the first incident.

September ended, and on the first Friday in October, the morning of the sixth-grade trip, fog cupped the windows and Gabe imagined himself to be in a cloud far above the treeline and mountains. He toyed with the idea of skipping school, but three thoughts nudged him from bed. The first two were that Webber and Mr. Boehm would be on the trip. And the third was the memory of his uncle's voice: "Don'tchu ever drop outta school. You get the ticket, hear me good. You ain't dumb like old Vernon. Git in gear."

Gabe dumped his backpack's contents on his desk. A couple of Smitty's cards, which he would sometimes take to school with him, tumbled out, and he hurriedly stuck them in one of his textbooks, like bookmarks. Then he put his bag lunch and the required pencil into his backpack. He had decided to read as many Tarzan books as the public library owned, and had checked out all five. He was now on the third one, which he put in his pack. Guppy watched Gabe with her usual motion-tracking as she sat on the plaid blanket rumpled on his bed. He kissed her behind her ears, ran his fingers backward up her spine to the dense mat of fur behind her neck, told her to be good, and walked to the front door. He looked back, his eyes sweeping from the study entrance to Guppy, still lying on the bed. He ran back to his room and hugged her fiercely around her neck and muscular shoulders.

Chapter 13

Gabe liked to read on the bus to school, and he was midswing with Tarzan when the bus jerked to a stop. He still read as he walked, jostled by other students, toward the orange Fullerton district buses in the school lot.

"I should have warned you about the stereotypes in those books," Mr. Boehm said, catching up to Gabe.

Gabe looked up at his teacher.

"Oh, yeah. You mean the natives?"

"Yes, the Africans. In Burroughs's time it was common to view Africans as stupid and primitive, without looking at them as individuals. Unfortunately, some people still do that."

"My uncle Vernon said sometimes you can tell a book by its cover."

The memory made Gabe half-smile.

"He said that?"

"Yeah, but he also said, 'I don't care what color a man's skin is. That don't matter one bit. It's what he does after the'—uh, I mean, 'after the you-know-what hits the fan. Does he go and fire live rounds into the sky like a crazy man? Does he take the C-rations off a dying buddy? Or does he tell that expectant that help is on the way and he done good? You think about it, Gabe. You think about it good and hard. You think about what you'd do after the gut-slopping shootin's done.' "

Gabe trembled and hung his head. *You don't talk like that to a teacher! And Mr. Boehm isn't even saying anything!*

Mr. Boehm squatted before Gabe, but when he placed his hands on Gabe's shoulders, the boy stiffened. Mr. Boehm let go, and spoke in a low voice.

"Gabe. Your uncle has nothing to worry about concerning what you'd do after the shooting's done. Of that I am certain."

Gabe didn't say anything, so Mr. Boehm continued.

"Okay, better find your bus. We've got a full day."

The clamor of kids teaming up for bus assignments overwhelmed the usual sixth-grade noise. With his high spirits, Webber had drawn a small crowd of students around him. He was thrilled. No sitting around all day, bored by the drone of teachers. Today would be pure fun, like playing hooky with permission. He jigged with excitement, unable to contain his energy. Mrs. Garvey reprimanded him even before he entered the bus.

"No banging on the bus, young man. We are not in the vicinity of a drum set."

He imitated her scolding when she turned, to the wild appreciation of his fellow students. When she turned back, she held a pale green demerit slip, demanded his name, inserted it on the proper line, and handed him the dreaded paper. The students instantly quieted. Webber was about to protest but met Mrs. Garvey's steel eyes and decided against it. Instead, he held back and complained to Gabe.

"Great, we have the wicked witch on our bus, plus Mrs. Sutherland—Janet's mother. She snorts louder than a tuba when she laughs—and she laughs all the time."

"I thought your mom was coming."

"She had to cancel—my grandma, you know. Mom's gonna love this demerit slip. . . . Jeez, they even make it the color of snot. My second one so far."

Webber shoved the slip into his pocket. The teacher and the parent chaperone stood at the bus door, clipboards in hand. As Webber and Gabe gave their names and boarded, Mrs. Sutherland let out a nasal laugh.

"Ho, ho, the famous Gable Pace, ho, hee-hee, ha."

Like a merry female Santa, she laughed, and her flesh quivered and her small blue eyes almost vanished beneath the mounds of her cheeks.

Gabe checked his zipper but couldn't figure out why he was the subject of Mrs. Sutherland's laughter. From inside the bus, he heard "Mother, puh-leeze!"

The boys shot aboard and settled into seats as far back as possible. Mrs. Garvey took attendance again, hammered home the rules, and bristled into a seat. Finally their bus left, the last of the three.

Early October in western Virginia trills with color shining through the clear air. White bands of clouds stripe the turquoise sky, patchwork farms and vineyards slope along hills in harvest shades and gilded green, and the mountain maples, northern red oak, and yellow birch begin to flare beside their evergreen neighbors. But none of this majesty mattered to the kids on the bus. The first time any of the students even noticed the outside world was the sighting of the five-pointed star on Mill Mountain above Roanoke as they neared their destination. Then all the kids crammed to the windows on that side of the bus and peered at the electric star. For the rest of the trip they argued about how many nights the famous star would be turned red if the bus plunged off the road, killing everyone.

As they left the bus at Center in the Square, each student received a worksheet to be completed in pencil as the day progressed. The first stop was the art museum and its traveling exhibit, "The Art of Nature, The Nature of Art." Students were allowed to pair off and go through the exhibit at their own pace, as long as they answered all the worksheet questions.

Janet was fascinated by the animal section, in particular the part on horses. There were paintings and drawings of horses, and an exhibit on the use of horse hair in brushes. She forced Brooke to spend most of the morning examining the horse pictures, from Appaloosas to Welsh ponies.

What interested Gabe was the northern tundra section. He liked the pure silver ice bowl decorated with polar bears, and the scrimshaw carved on ancient ivory. But what he really liked the most was the case filled with Jack London's Klondike writings and manuscripts, loaned from Pasadena's Huntington Library.

"Wow, Webber. He actually wrote that. His very own diary."

"Come on, slowpoke. Charley said the marble floor is so shiny in the next room you can see up dresses."

"None of the girls wear dresses. I ain't interested in seeing Mrs. Garvey's underwear. . . . I sure would like to touch it."

"Touch her underwear?"

"No, goof. The diary."

"Well, maybe there's a way. . . ." Webber started pushing on the glass case.

"Webber, stop! Okay, I'm coming. You satisfied? Good grief, you want to get us arrested?"

The boys scribbled on their worksheets as they shuffled off to the next room to join Charley, who was angling his head this way and that.

The mild day allowed the students to eat lunch outside in Market Square. When Gabe opened his backpack, he found a paper folded inside. He felt his heart heave. The note was not in its customary envelope, nor on its customary card, but just the same, Gabe looked around to see if now, at long last, Smitty would appear. He heard a dog bark and his head snapped in the direction of the sound. But it was a little snippet dog, a papillon straining its skinny neck at a leash on the far side of the square. Gabe felt the paper ripped from his hand and, startled, he raced after Brooke, who held the note high over her head.

"Give that back!" he yelled.

"Yeah, who wants it? Who wants it bad? Oh, how romantic, young adolescent love, Janet and—"

Gabe stopped running. "Oh," he said. "Oh, okay." And he walked away.

Janet, her single braid whipping the side of her head, snatched her note and seethed at Brooke. "Some friend. Thanks a million. For nothing."

While Webber urged Gabe to finish his sandwich quickly so they could play Frisbee, Gabe noticed Janet sitting by herself, her face still splotched. When her mother walked toward her, Janet moved to sit with Lucinda and Anneka for the rest of the lunch break.

The afternoon planetarium show, "Night Wonders: The Aurora Borealis and Other Spectacles," gave everyone a chance to sink into armchair comfort. Even Webber relaxed his high-spin energy in the lull of the dark and the spectral play of light. When dawn crept up the dome at the end of the show and the students focused on the great antlike celestial projector whirring in the center, Janet found a note in her lap, which she quickly read and hid.

I would like to read your note sometime.
—G.C.P.

The students were herded back on the buses, and, as before, Mrs. Garvey's lecture on proper behavior for the bus ride slowed the departure of her busload of charges. The noise level on Gabe's bus was initially low, but it increased steadily as they rode. When it reached a certain pitch, Mrs. Garvey carefully stood up, braced her knee firmly in her seat, and turned to face the children. Unfortunately, the movement caused Webber to turn his head, and the spitball from his straw, aimed at Charley, glued itself instead to Mrs. Garvey's nose.

Webber found himself with another "snot-colored" demerit slip, a public dressing-down, and the promise that his parents and the vice-principal in charge of discipline would be thoroughly informed of his misbehavior. The noise level on the bus rarely reached above a loud hum after that, until the bus creaked into the school lane.

"Oh my God, Webber is in so much trouble."

"Holy moly. She must have called ahead on a cell phone."

"Don't be ridiculous, it was a spitball, not a bullet. Maybe he did something else. You know Webber."

These comments were whispered, shot across the bus like so many darts. Because waiting in the school parking lot were not only the other two buses and the rest of the students, but also three police and sheriff vehicles, one with its lights still flashing. Several kids on Gabe's bus identified Mrs. Pickering, rubbing her arms and standing on the curb by the vice-principal. Near them, gesturing angrily in front of an officer and the principal, pointing at the police cars and the incoming bus, was Mr. Boehm.

The windows along the inside of the bus were plastered with every student's face, smushed against the panes, trying to see everything as the bus parked. Gabe was pushed against the window by Webber and several other boys. Meanwhile, Janet's fingers flicked the edge of her note. She was determined to give it to Gabe.

The bus driver cranked open the door and admitted the man who had just been arguing with Mr. Boehm. The county sheriff, a balding man in his sixties whose sallow skin blended with his beige uniform, called from the front of the bus.

"Gable Pace, come here."

Gabe had tried to shrink into nothingness as soon as he saw the police cars. Only he had understood immediately why the police were there, and yet everything around him seemed to warp into a filmy dream. All the faces staring at him were blurred as he stumbled by Webber's knees. Gabe put his head down and clutched his pack in front of him. After he passed Janet's seat, she dropped her hand, the message undeliverable. Sheriff Aiden Hewitt put a sweaty hand on Gabe's shoulder at the base of his neck, and the two stepped off the bus, like a little tugboat tethered to its ungainly barge.

Gabe heard his name twice: "Gabe, honey!" called by Mrs. Pickering and "Gabe!" called by Mr. Boehm with the urgent, sharp tone of warning. Gabe looked up, twisted from the sheriff's grasp, and ran the length of the bus. He sprinted across the parking lot, running as fast and as hard as he could. An officer in chase caught a strap of his backpack, and Gabe let go of the bag.

When he was caught, at the edge of the lot, Gabe kicked and punched wildly, stabbing the air randomly. Officers tried to calm him, but he was frantic. When his arm was brought behind his back and he was lifted from the ground, he wrenched his body as if he didn't care if his arm broke.

"My God, let him go! He's a little boy! He'll hurt himself. I told you this was not the way to do this." Mr. Boehm worked his way into the circle of police. "Please, just let me talk to him."

Mr. Boehm squatted before Gabe, who was still being restrained.

"Gabe, they only want to talk to you. You can do that. Everything will work out. Come on, Gabe, just take a deep breath. It's okay. They found your uncle's body—you have to talk to them."

Gabe stopped writhing and fell limp. The officers put him on his feet, and he collapsed before Mr. Boehm.

"I didn't do it," Gabe whimpered.

"Of course not, no, nobody thinks you did."

Gabe looked up to see Mr. Boehm glaring at the sheriff. Then he heard Mrs. Pickering's familiar voice.

"Let me through! He's my son's best friend. And I'm his emergency contact, just ask the principal. I'm coming, Gabe!"

Gabe turned white as Mrs. Pickering spoke, and he felt the sheriff's eyes drilling into him. Gabe suddenly leaned in toward Mr. Boehm and whispered, "I have to get home. Guppy needs me!"

"I think you have to go with these officers first," Mr. Boehm said, as gently as possible.

"You have to help me. It's a secret. I have a secret dog. She needs to be fed. And I have a secret friend, Smitty. He might take care of Guppy, I don't know. Please, please, say you'll do it!"

"Okay, Gabe. I'll do my best."

Gabe's voice, in the heat of the moment, had not been as quiet as he had hoped.

"Son, you don't have any secrets anymore. You understand?" said the sheriff. "We're going into the station now. I don't want any more trouble."

"Be gentle! Please!" said Mr. Boehm.

"We'll do what we need to do to keep the community safe," Hewitt replied, hitching his belt. "We're on the same side, remember?"

Gabe, gripped more firmly by the sheriff, surrounded by officers and trailed by Mrs. Pickering, Webber, and the vice-principal, was guided to the backseat of the deputy's car.

Chapter 14

Gabe sat in a small room in the police station. It was paneled with flimsy, warped particle board and lit by a yellowed light fixture that held years' worth of captured dead insects.

Gabe sat very still on his chair as he struggled to answer Sheriff Hewitt's questions. Mrs. Pickering had been in the room too, until, very early in the questioning, Sheriff Hewitt had asked Gabe if his uncle had indeed listed her on the school forms. When Gabe admitted that he'd been the one to fill in her name, Mrs. Pickering, protesting all the way, was escorted to the station's lobby to join her son. The sheriff then barked at the vice-principal to get the previous year's forms and get them quick! She ran out in a hurry. Left in the room were Gabe, the sheriff, and Mr. Yancy, a child psychologist from Child Protective Services.

Mr. Yancy had a glass eye and was seemingly able to direct his gaze at Gabe and the sheriff at the same time, even when the sheriff stood on the far side of the room. Every time Mr. Yancy nodded, Gabe and the sheriff each thought the nod was for him, and they got confused. Finally, Gabe simply looked at his own lap.

"So tell me, Gabe—right, you prefer Gabe?" the sheriff asked, and Gabe nodded. "Tell me again, so I have it straight, what happened when you came home from school that first day."

"I came in the door and I saw my uncle laying on the floor and he wasn't moving or nothing, and I was scared 'cause his fan was on the floor too, like it was knocked over."

Gabe thought he was going to have to repeat everything again, so he was surprised by the next question.

"And your uncle's guns. When did you notice they were gone?"

"Uh, they're gone? He told me never to touch his guns."

Why hadn't he checked the guns! Gabe's thoughts rushed around his head like leaves blown before the wind.

"And your uncle's body. Tell me again where it went."

"I don't know. It was just gone—the next day." Would

he be forced to admit just how dumb he felt? That he had believed he had a fairy godmother? But the sheriff asked a different sort of question.

"Did you ever visit the Dillard Mortuary—the funeral home?"

"Uh, no."

"And how about Mr. Smith?"

"I, uh, Mr. Smith?"

The sheriff looked steadily at Gabe and asked, "Might have called himself Smitty?"

Gabe's eyes widened as he realized the sheriff knew a lot more than he had been letting on. If only the sheriff would tell him that Guppy and Smitty were fine!

"Yes, the embalmer at the mortuary," continued the sheriff. "He fixed up your uncle's body. Perfectly preserved. Found by Mr. Dillard today in the basement of the mortuary. Don't play dumb with me."

"No, sir. It's just that, well, I know Smitty, um, sort of know him. But I didn't know what he did."

"He didn't take you to where he worked?"

"No, um, I never met him."

"Really? Hmm. Now, Gabe," said the sheriff, as if he had all the time in the world, "I think the question we all want answered, and answered straight, is why you didn't call the police when you found your uncle, or then, when you found his body was gone."

Gabe was silent until the sheriff prompted him again.

"Did Mr. Smith threaten you, make you keep quiet?"

"No, no!" Gabe quickly replied. But his confused memories became jumbled with the new information about his uncle's body. He couldn't really explain why he hadn't sought help. Official help.

"He must have scared you, though. . . ."

"No, well, sort of. Sometimes."

The sheriff said, "Yes? That he would hurt you?"

"Not really. I, um, got scared of the mailbox."

The sheriff sighed in exasperation and changed tactics.

"Tell me again, Gabe, where did you find the big black dog?"

Gabe breathed in sharply, gathered his courage, and this time asked his own questions.

"Is she here too? Can I see her?"

"No, she's not here," said the sheriff testily. "She ever bite anyone? Act vicious?"

"N-no, sir."

"You're sure? You don't sound too convincing."

"She don't bite."

"But she acts vicious? Right?"

"Only when the postman comes on Saturday." Gabe looked up with his dark eyes right on the sheriff. "Please, she's just afraid of him. She didn't . . ." Gabe pictured Guppy surrounded by police, like being surrounded by a dozen postmen. He bowed his head again, rocked on his chair, and twitched his mouth. Mr. Yancy suggested a break.

Sheriff Hewitt stretched his legs and opened the door. One of his clerks stood there and started talking rapidly.

"Sheriff, the newspeople are asking for an interview but I told them they couldn't bring their news cameras in here—so they're setting up by the flagpole outside."

The sheriff grunted, and the clerk continued at top speed. "Then there's a very pushy teacher who just came and he won't take no, keeps saying he needs to see the boy. Oh, and Detective Lynch from the county jail up in Toulom wants to talk with you again, and the coroner's office, oh, and the vice-principal called and I took down all the information, and then Animal Control Services—"

"All right, all right, Clarice, shush and slow down, let me out of the room, will you, and get Lynch on the phone."

The door closed, leaving Mr. Yancy and Gabe alone.

"How are you holding up?" asked Mr. Yancy. His glass eye seemed to get restless when he talked.

"Fine," Gabe mumbled.

After a silence, Mr. Yancy said, "You're safe now."

Safe! Gabe didn't think he could feel less safe.

When Mrs. Garvey stepped into the small back room, Gabe sat up straight. Maybe she would give him so many demerit slips they would have to send him to jail. *No, that's not right! Where's Guppy? Smitty!*

The sheriff had followed Mrs. Garvey in. She took one look at Gabe and motioned for the sheriff to come back into the hall. In a few minutes, the door reopened. Mrs. Garvey pointed a straight-arrow finger at Gabe.

"You will not run away again, young man. Will you?"

"No, ma'am," he said, still as a stone.

"You see, Aiden. I will not have you sending this boy to Juvenile Hall. Ulysses and I can give him all the protection he needs."

"Ulysses? As in *Judge* Ulysses Garvey?" asked Mr.

Yancy. "You're Mrs. Garvey?" His eye bobbled in approval, and Mrs. Garvey gave a brief nod.

But Sheriff Aiden Hewitt protested, "Aw, Octavia. That's not protocol."

"Protocol? Is there a protocol for a boy who lost his uncle? This student writes down every word I say. That is not the behavior of a 'flight risk,' as you term him. Now, have you even given the poor boy something to eat? I thought not. We shall depart. You know where to find him. Come, Gabe."

Gabe raised his hand just above his ear.

"Yes?" asked Mrs. Garvey.

"Can I use the bathroom?"

"Really, now, Aiden. You see?" Mrs. Garvey turned to Gabe. "Of course you can."

Flight risk, huh, thought Gabe. *Yes, flying away would be perfect now.* If only he could! He'd find Guppy and Smitty and fly away. Like magic. It happened in books! But not all books—Lennie couldn't fly away when he was in trouble. Gabe stumbled out of the room.

When Gabe came out of the men's room, he saw Mrs. Garvey talking with Mr. Boehm and Mrs. Pickering at the end of the hall. But when Webber shouted, "Gabe-man!" Mrs. Garvey ended the discussion abruptly. She opened the door to the lobby and ushered the three out. Gabe could see a camera flash and Mr. Boehm rubbing his eyes. Mrs. Garvey closed the lobby door quickly and took Gabe and his backpack out the rear exit of the building.

Chapter 15

Mrs. Garvey looked approvingly at Gabe as he ate the leftover meat loaf coated with tomato paste. Gabe smiled back weakly. Gabe and Mr. and Mrs. Garvey sat at the hexagonal table in the sunroom next to the kitchen. If Mrs. Garvey was like a steel needle, her husband was more like a haystack—pleasingly round and inviting.

"You see, Tavie," teased the judge, "not all children hide their portion of your famous meat loaf under a napkin."

"Now stop that, Ulysses, or you'll find yourself cooking your own meals."

Mr. Garvey winked at Gabe, then whispered, "Always

let the woman have the last word. That will keep you out of a whole lot of trouble."

Mrs. Garvey? A woman? Gabe had never thought about that. She was a teacher. And yet here she was talking about things that had nothing to do with math. And, as the photographs on the mantel and shelves proved, she was a mother! A grandmother! Gabe wasn't sure he really wanted to think about it, but since his mind kept racing anyway, at least it was something different.

"What are you two up to?" Mrs. Garvey demanded.

"Oh, just giving Gabe a little advice on women." Mr. Garvey turned to Gabe. "You have a girlfriend yet?"

Gabe blushed. "N-no," he stammered.

"Oh-ho. Someone you've got your eye on, though, right?"

"Will you leave the poor child alone?"

Gabe paused, then leaned over and whispered, "Yes," to Mr. Garvey.

"Ohh!" said Mr. Garvey with a laugh. When his wife again demanded the cause of all the whispering, he winked once more at Gabe, buttoned his lip, and rose to clear the table.

The doorbell and phone rang several times while "the men" cleaned the kitchen, and Gabe could hear Mrs. Garvey say, "We are a private residence and have no comment. Do not call again," over and over.

Mr. Garvey was showing Gabe home videos of fishing with the grandkids when Mr. Boehm entered the den.

Gabe popped up from his chair, energized by the unexpected visit.

"Hi, Mr. Boehm," he said.

"Hey, Gabe, how's it going?"

"Okay."

The Garveys encouraged their guests to make themselves comfortable, then left the room.

"I hear you're watching a fishing video," said Mr. Boehm.

"Yeah. Mr. Garvey said he would show me his gear tomorrow."

"That sounds fine. . . ."

Gabe perched anxiously at the edge of his seat. He was desperate to ask a million questions—about Smitty, and his uncle's body, and most of all, about Guppy.

"I know you asked me to look after Guppy—did the sheriff tell you anything about her?"

"No!" Gabe could hardly breathe.

"Okay, don't worry, she's okay, but she does have an injury. They're taking care of her at Animal Control Services. They gave me a copy of her intake picture. Here it is—for you."

Gabe clutched the picture. He rubbed his nose against his shirtsleeve without taking his eyes from the photo. Guppy's head and shoulders filled most of the picture, her long snout resting on a cement floor, her eyes closed, fur matted.

"She's okay, all right?" said Mr. Boehm. "I'd like to tell you what happened, though. Would that be okay with you?"

Gabe nodded. Of course it was okay. She was alive!

"It's like this," said Mr. Boehm. "Sometimes people become scared that a dog is going to do something dangerous. Big dogs can be scary. Some people are scared of my dog, and he wouldn't hurt anyone."

"Guppy can be scary when she barks," Gabe whispered. "But she hardly ever barks, 'cept when she's scared."

"Well, see, that's probably what happened. The police came to your house, she became scared, then she scared the police with her barking, and the police officer became scared. He thought she was going to attack him, so he shot her—"

"She was shot!"

"Yes, but remember, she's okay. The leg's pretty bad, though."

Gabe wished Guppy were by his side, sprawled on the rug, waiting for a tummy rub. Guppy knew how to make him feel safe. How could he let her get shot! *And in the leg—she loves to run!* Gabe looked at his own leg just as his teacher leaned forward to give Gabe's knee a comforting pat. Mr. Boehm quickly withdrew his hand.

"I'm going to go out to my car and get the things I picked up from your house," said Mr. Boehm.

Gabe waited with the Garveys inside their front door for Mr. Boehm to return with the box.

"Mr. Boehm?" asked Gabe.

"Yes, Gabe."

"Can I see her?"

"Guppy? Well, I think it's better to wait a little until she feels better. Do you think you can do that?"

"Okay."

"Okay, then." Mr. Boehm turned to Mrs. Garvey. "Thank you so much, Octavia. May I call again?"

"Certainly, Hank."

"Thanks. Goodnight. Goodnight, Gabe."

"G'night, Mr. Boehm."

Mr. Boehm held out his hand. But Gabe did not take it, and again Mr. Boehm found himself squatting before the boy.

"Gabe," said Mr. Boehm, "if there is anything you need, anything you want, please just let me know. Anything at all."

"Thanks for the picture," whispered Gabe. "And, um, I was wondering if Smitty is okay."

"Honestly, I'm not sure. He's not hurt, if that's what you mean. The police need to talk with him some more, though." Mr. Boehm paused and cast his eyes downward. "Look, Gabe, I can find a good lawyer for him, don't worry. My father knows many, many lawyers." Gabe waited while Mr. Boehm looked off to the side for a moment. Finally, Mr. Boehm said, "For now, Mr. Smith is at the county jail, up at Toulom. That's all I know."

That was enough for Gabe for the night. That and the plaid blanket. Mr. Garvey carried Gabe's belongings upstairs and showed the boy his room. The Garveys called goodnight from the doorway, and after they left, Gabe rubbed his cheek against the smooth surface of Guppy's photo. He slid under the blanket and fell immediately into a troubled sleep.

Chapter 16

Late the next morning, after both the detective and Sheriff Hewitt had stopped by to question Gabe some more, Mr. Boehm returned to the Garvey household. Tired and numb from the questioning, Gabe barely spoke to his teacher. Mr. Boehm left after only a brief visit.

That afternoon, Webber, still in his soccer uniform and bouncy from his latest victory, arrived with his mother. As Gabe and Webber went up together to the guest room, Webber peered curiously around the halls and doorways, amazed that a teacher, and in particular Mrs. Garvey, lived in what looked like a normal house.

Webber picked up various knickknacks from the guest

room bureau; then, tossing up a glass paperweight, he turned to Gabe.

"Sorry 'bout your uncle, man."

"Thanks."

"They're saying you've been living by yourself, huh?"

"No, not really. I was with Guppy. Here's her picture."

"Lucky! I mean, uh—"

"Well, she's not really mine. Sort of a loaner dog, I guess."

"Oh. . . . But how come you didn't . . . I mean, I'm your best friend, but you never . . ."

Gabe looked at his hands.

Webber was not used to silences and quickly asked, "Want me to tell you about the game? Well, right off they try some feeble attempt at goal, and Joaquin passes me the ball and I dribble it all the way down the *center* of the field! The other team sucked! They're called the Lancers, but you wanna hear what I call them?"

"The Losers?"

"The L—Yeah, that's it."

Webber heard his mother call him from the bottom of the stairs. He spun the paperweight at Gabe, who barely caught it. At the guest room door, Webber turned and said, "Yeah, well, I don't tell you everything either."

After Webber left, Gabe found a piece of paper and a pen in the guest room desk and wrote:

> *Dear Smitty,*
>   *I'm sorry I got you in so much trouble.*
> *Guppy is*

But then he stopped. How could he tell Smitty that Guppy was hurt? Gabe started crossing out that part, then wound up crossing everything out, over and over. Then he tore the note up into tiny bits and hid the bits under the mattress.

He went to bed early. "G'night, Uncle Vernon," he whispered.

The next day, Mrs. Pickering phoned instead of visiting.

Gabe, unused to talking on a phone, barely said a word to her. She handed the phone to Webber.

"Sorry," Gabe started.

Webber didn't need an apology. Rather, he needed to unload.

"It's a royal pain in the B-U-T-T having your baby sister poke in all your stuff," he told Gabe. "You're lucky you don't have a sister. Annie had to move in with me last night 'cause Grandma moved into Annie's room. And we have to be really quiet all the time. I wish my dad would let me move in with him. Though I dunno about living with Mrs. Garvey. That's freakazoid, man. But hey—I have a solution! My grandma can move in with Mrs. Garvey and you can come live with us! That would be perfect."

Gabe gave a small laugh, looked over at Mrs. Garvey, and said he had to go. Move in with Webber—how often had he wished it!

Later that afternoon, Gabe had a visitor he both dreaded and welcomed. Ms. Rodriguez had made a special trip from Richmond.

"Gabe, I'm not going to grill you with questions. I imagine you're sick of questions by now."

Gabe didn't reply. The back of his neck prickled whenever someone sat him down at the mahogany dining room table for a talk.

"I'm going to tell you a little story instead," said Ms. Rodriguez. "About one of my home visits when you were at school. Oh yes, some of the trips were just to see Vernon. It must have been less than six months after I took you to his house. Once he finished cussing about my ruining his day, you know what he said? 'Ms. R,' he said, 'you was right about that boy.' I just stood there—he had a hangdog look, like he was making a confession to a priest. 'Yes,' he said, 'that boy's given me more'n I'll ever give him. If the Lord strikes me down tomorrow, at least I'll know I warn't put here fer nuthin'. I'll know there's a good 'n' decent Culligan left on earth.' "

Gabe's shoulders heaved and his bowed head rocked on his crossed arms. "But I'm not good and decent," Gabe moaned. "I lied to you. I lied about Uncle Vernon."

"Gabe, look at me."

After he raised his blotchy face, Ms. Rodriguez continued. "I know you don't feel good about yourself right now. But do you know who did the most lying that night? . . . Me. I lied to myself. I thought something was wrong the moment I knocked on the door. But I just lied to myself. I didn't want anything to ruin your placement. And so I pretended that everything was okay. I came up with the best explanation I could at the time—that Vernon didn't want to see me and was just waiting outside till I left—and I didn't probe any deeper. I'm having a hard time living with myself right now."

"You are?"

"Yes, but you know what's keeping me going? I think about old Vernon."

"Me too!"

"You know, I think he'd be pretty proud of you making it on your own."

"Really?"

"Oh yes. Time and again I told him to set up a guardian for you should anything happen to him. He did not want you going back into the foster system. That's the last thing he wanted. But he just couldn't seem to deal with the thought of losing you in any way."

Gabe winced at the mention of foster care, and a silence stretched between them.

"Gabe?"

"Thanks," he said at last.

"Thanks? For what?"

"Well, um, thanks for thinking about Uncle Vernon. Sometimes I think that people in heaven are lonesome unless someone down here thinks about 'em. And even though I think about him a lot, and so does Smitty, I like that someone else is thinking about him."

"Ah, Smitty. Paul Smith."

"Yes," said Gabe excitedly. "You know him?"

"No. Everyone's talking about him, though. Did he hurt you?"

"Hurt me? No—he helped me! Nobody'll tell me if he's okay. Even Mr. Boehm said he wasn't sure. And he's the only one who'll tell me anything."

"Mr. Boehm?"

"Knock, knock. I think my ears are burning." Mr. Boehm rapped his knuckles on the wooden archway to the dining room and rubbed one of his long-lobed ears. "Mrs. Garvey said you were both in here. Pardon my intrusion. Hello, Ms. Rodriguez, I'm Hank Boehm."

He shook Maria Rodriguez's hand and tipped his head in a brief bow.

"Hi, Mr. Boehm!" said Gabe.

"My, you're in better spirits. It looks like Ms. Rodriguez has done you a world of good. I thought you might still be sad, so I brought a surprise for you."

"Guppy!"

"Well, no, Guppy is still recovering."

Gabe's hopes crumbled and Mr. Boehm hastily continued: "I brought my dog instead. Mrs. Garvey let me tie him up out back. His name's Tiresias, if you want to go meet him."

Tiresias was sitting under a purpleleaf plum tree. His leash was loosely tied to a wrought-iron chair. He shuffled to his feet at Gabe's approach. Gray fur was mixed with blond, especially on Tiresias's snout. His eyes held milky clouds, which Gabe thought made the dog seem as if he were always looking at the beginnings of galaxies. Gabe stroked Tiresias's long fur, then wrapped his arms around him.

"Hey, boy, whatcha been up to? You a good dog? You

sure are." Gabe ran back inside and asked Mrs. Garvey for a bowl to give the dog water.

"Of course. But don't come tracking that dog hair in this house."

Gabe froze and looked down at his shirt.

"Now, now," reassured Mrs. Garvey. "That's all right, go play with him."

Gabe carried the bowl out and continued to talk with the dog but this time didn't hug him. He did, though, scratch behind Tiresias's soft dun ears.

"Oh, you like that, don't you. Good boy. What else do you like, huh? I bet you like Mr. Boehm. Yeah, good dog. Good, good dog."

But even to Tiresias, Gabe couldn't voice his innermost thoughts. How could he ever say what he truly, truly wanted? He lowered his head, wrapped his arms around his stomach, and mumbled to himself. After several minutes, he rose, looked hard at the dog, and ran back to the house. He ran by Mrs. Garvey in the kitchen, Mr. Garvey in the den, and Mr. Boehm and Ms. Rodriguez in the dining room. So many grown-ups in one house! He ran up to the guest room and flung himself onto the bed.

Chapter 17

When Mrs. Garvey pulled her car into the staff parking lot early Monday morning, she turned to Gabe. He clutched the armrest.

"Gabe, this may be another hard day for you," said Mrs. Garvey, "but you are to go to school nonetheless. Those news reporters out there aren't allowed on school property, so you needn't worry. Meet me in my room immediately after the final bell, do you understand?"

"Yessum." If only the final bell were right now!

When Gabe did not move, she asked, "Do you have your lunch?"

"Yessum."

"Then why, pray tell, are you still sitting here?"

"I, um, forgot my books." Without looking up at her, Gabe shook his near-empty backpack. "I, uh, didn't bring them on the trip Friday. They're still at home, on my desk. And I, well, I didn't want to bother you, and—"

Mrs. Garvey smoothed her light wool skirt. "I see," she said slowly. "But I don't believe your books could be on your desk. Surely Mr. Boehm would have seen them when he picked up your clothes." She added, "Oh, bother! I know what must have happened. Don't worry, I'm sure we can get them for you."

And so Gabe suffered a deep humiliation that day at school. Not due to the photographer who climbed the fence and tracked Gabe with his telephoto lens. Not due to Janet in homeroom, who busied herself in a notebook after Gabe said hi. Not due to the morning break he spent in the first-floor boys' bathroom, avoiding whispers, stares, and his new nickname, Dead Man. But later, during English class, well after the students were done teasing Mr. Boehm about his new, clean-shaven look.

The humiliation occurred halfway through the class, when a box of items taken from Gabe's desk at home by the sheriff's department on Friday was returned to him. Despite taunts—"Special delivery, Mr. Pace, paging Mr. Pace"—from his classmates, taunts quickly silenced by Mr. Boehm, Gabe refused to open the box during class. After everyone ran from the room at the bell, as usual, Gabe began to empty the marked and tagged box, shoving its contents into his backpack. When he reached the bottom of his pile of books, he found his mother's picture staring up at him. Her face, framed by the stiff cardboard leaves of the box, made him feel more hurt in one split second than at any other time in his life. His special drawer! They'd gone into his secret and precious things! His stomach twisted as if a hand were squeezing his insides. He did not realize he had cried out until Mr. Boehm stood suddenly by his side.

"Gabe, what is it?"

Gabe panted and grunted, searching for words to name this new hurt. "They went . . . They took . . ." A moment later, he found the words—they had been written weeks before on a cream-colored card just for him. Gabe shouted at Mr. Boehm in anger.

"They're not honoring the memory! They're not honoring the memory of Uncle Vernon. That's what Smitty said to do, and they're not doin' it! They're not! And where's Smitty? I want Smitty! Smitty's my friend! Why doesn't anyone believe me? I need to warn him! Be careful or they'll get your stuff too!"

Gabe feverishly withdrew a piece of paper from his pack and began writing a note. When he looked up, he saw a ring of eighth graders staring at him. Mr. Boehm shooed them to their seats and made a phone call. Gabe shoved his belongings into his pack and, wild-eyed, started toward the door.

"No, Gabe, wait!" Mr. Boehm called.

After Ms. Tsang hurried into the room, Mr. Boehm said, "Come with me, Gabe. Let's do this right."

They first stopped at Mrs. Garvey's room, and Gabe waited in the hall, tense and pacing, for Mr. Boehm to come out again. Then Mr. Boehm signed himself and Gabe out of school and they settled in Mr. Boehm's Jeep. Gabe, though, twitched about and had to be reminded to put on his seat belt. Mr. Boehm gave him a choice: did he want to see Smitty or not?

"Uh, see Smitty? Like really see him?"

"To be honest, Gabe, I don't know if they allow children to visit at the Toulom county jail." Then Mr. Boehm suddenly turned to Gabe. "That's not what you meant, though, is it?"

"No." Gabe was quiet. He wished he could dissolve into one of the mists that cloaked the mountains. The prospect of actually meeting Smitty frightened him almost as much as the barred and clanging jail block he pictured. Would Smitty lash out at Gabe for getting him in trouble? The air around Gabe seemed to fill with angry black slashes.

"It's true, then, that you've never seen Smitty?"

"Never."

"Ah . . . Perhaps we should turn back."

"No, no, please!"

"Mrs. Garvey wanted to protect you. But I thought that sooner or later you would know anyway. The newspeople are going wild with the whole thing—I don't think there's an angle they've missed. Even mentioned my father! As for me, I couldn't believe someone whom you had never met would mean so much to you. Poor fellow."

Gabe was lost, though "poor fellow" he recognized. "Why is he a poor fellow?" Gabe asked.

Mr. Boehm winced. "I've never seen him, mind you.

Not many people have, apparently. He lives in a cottage behind the funeral home and he works in the mortuary basement. Mr. Dillard said Mr. Smith is the best embalmer in all of western Virginia—he preserves dead bodies with chemicals. It's a normal part of burial."

Gabe nodded, so Mr. Boehm continued, "Nobody understands why he kept your uncle's body, why he left you in the house by yourself. But he seems to be a reclusive fellow—likes to be alone. And if you see his picture printed in the paper, you'll understand why." Mr. Boehm looked over at Gabe before he finished. "Part of his face is missing. A large part. I'm sorry."

Gabe thought about this new information. Some time ago he had figured out that his uncle and Smitty knew each other from the Vietnam War, and he grimaced, thinking about a bomb or grenade injuring his uncle's friend.

"Gabe?"

The boy turned to his teacher; then, blushing slightly, he smiled.

"What, Gabe? Why are you smiling?"

"Because I feel better. Thanks for telling me about Smitty. Now I get it. I don't think he would want me to see him. But maybe he'll take a note. That's what we're used to, anyway." As Mr. Boehm still looked quizzical at his grin, Gabe continued. "I was just thinking about the time Webber asked me if Uncle Vernon was ugly— Webber wanted my uncle to marry his mom so we could be brothers. I wanted that too. Real bad. Only problem was, Uncle Vernon was already dead." Gabe looked shyly up at Mr. Boehm.

"That would put a damper on a wedding ceremony, I expect. Well, that is a weird image." Mr. Boehm smiled too.

"Yeah, but Smitty told me that thinking weird things is okay. It doesn't mean I'm bad."

"I'm really getting to like Smitty."

Mr. Boehm parked his Jeep in a Visitors Only slot, then walked with Gabe through the metal detectors. Mr. Boehm explained to the receptionist that they wanted to leave a note for Mr. Paul R. Smith. The receptionist took their names and made a phone call to the back. A young deputy came and guided Gabe and Mr. Boehm to a bench outside the sheriff's office. The deputy stood stiff as a royal guard.

"I feel like I've been sent to the principal's office," whispered Mr. Boehm. Gabe giggled but abruptly stopped when the door swung open and Sheriff Aiden Hewitt's husky form filled the doorway.

"What in the world are you thinking, Boehm, bringing that boy here?"

"Yes, that is a good question, sir," said Mr. Boehm quickly. "He hasn't been told much, you see. He was surprised, I believe, when some of the items secured by the police—some of his books and belongings—were returned to him during English class this morning. And, well, I hated to see him upset again."

"So bringing him here is going to calm him down?"

"He's very worried about Mr. Smith. They are friends and had a correspondence. Gabe wanted to leave him a note."

"I see. Well, I'm glad to see that at least you've calmed

down. Cleaned up a bit too, eh? But leaving a note for Mr. Smith? That would be difficult."

"Yes, sir."

"For one thing, Mr. Smith is no longer here."

Gabe opened his mouth in surprise.

"You can both come into my office," the sheriff offered. "You too, Johnson," Hewitt commanded his junior staff member. "I may need you to fetch some files for me."

Sheriff Hewitt had the largest desk Gabe had ever seen. Gabe found himself staring at the little American and State of Virginia flags at either end of the sheriff's nameplate.

"Gable. I mean, Gabe."

Gabe looked up at the sheriff, who pointed at him. "You're a fine young man."

Gabe didn't say anything till Mr. Boehm twitched his head and furrowed his brow slightly.

"Uh, thank you, sir."

"Do you know, Boehm, what this young man did while he lived on his own?"

Mr. Boehm shook his head. When Gabe twitched his eyebrows, Mr. Boehm cleared his throat and said, "No, sir, I do not."

"For one thing, he kept a shipshape house. But that's not all. He kept a tally of all the money he took from his uncle's cash box—every cent, it seems. He called the tally 'Money Gabe Owes Uncle Vernon.' Isn't that remarkable? In this day and age?"

"Yes, most remarkable. Though, to be honest, I am not surprised."

"Right." Hewitt turned to Gabe. "You're worried about your friend. I can understand that. You and he had quite a nice little 'correspondence,' as your teacher says. Lots of cards and letters."

Gabe felt the heat rising in his chest, and he moved to the edge of his chair.

The sheriff continued. "That correspondence, as well as your uncle's letters to him, is why he's no longer here."

"You released him?" asked Mr. Boehm.

"Now, don't jump to conclusions. The coroner sent in his first report this morning, which said there was no sign of wrongdoing. Mr. Culligan died of natural causes. Heart attack. Lungs and liver weren't too good either."

The sheriff paused a moment and looked at Gabe. "You okay with this, son?" When Gabe nodded, Sheriff Hewitt continued. "Furthermore, the letters from Mr. Culligan, kept by Mr. Smith, indicate that Mr. Culligan did not want his nephew returned to foster care. The DA feels that Mr. Smith, under the circumstances, did the best he could to honor what he thought were Mr. Culligan's wishes. So, for instance, we now think he removed Mr. Culligan's guns from the house and kept them with Mr. Culligan's body so the boy wouldn't accidentally hurt himself. We believe Mr. Smith merely wanted Gabe to have some extra time to figure things out. Not exactly the decision I would have made, but then, what we're trying to weigh is if he broke the law. We haven't dropped all charges against him yet, but he didn't need to be here."

"Could you tell us, Sheriff, where is Mr. Smith?" asked Mr. Boehm.

"He's at a hospital, the veterans' hospital in Salem."

Gabe stiffened. *A hospital! Oh no! They shot him, too!*

Sheriff Hewitt quickly added, "He's fine, he's just, er, upset. He's on the psychiatric ward. He's been there before, son. He needs some rest. They know him and will take good care of him."

The fresh-faced deputy standing behind the sheriff grinned a gap-toothed smile and rocked on his heels.

"Do you have something to add to the conversation, Deputy Johnson?"

"Yep," said the deputy, "he's been there before. All the officers been talking 'bout it. He's been there, all right."

Mr. Boehm said hastily, "I don't think that needs to be public knowledge." The sheriff added his warning as well: "Careful now, Johnson."

But the deputy blurted out, "Like after the time he took a rifle and—" The deputy pointed a pretend gun at his own face.

Gabe fell from his chair, clutching his stomach.

Chapter 18

The next morning was overcast. While Mr. Boehm read the spelling list aloud, Gabe gazed out the window at the gray clouds. When Mr. Boehm came to the word "commitment," Gabe could feel his teacher's eyes upon him. At the end of class, Mr. Boehm strode to Gabe's chair. But Gabe, as usual, took his time collecting his books.

Gabe had been taken directly to Mr. Yancy's office after the disastrous trip to the Toulom county jail the day before, and he thought his teacher might be angry that he hadn't said a word to Mr. Yancy. Was Mr. Boehm going to give him more bad news?

"I'll be picking up Guppy from the vet's today. The

veterinarian said the woman from the Humane Society did such a good job that Guppy's leg is going to be okay."

Gabe felt a rush of relief, like taking his first breath after a long underwater swim. "She's got all four legs?"

"Yes, but she's still weak, I expect, and I thought it might be best for her to get stronger before you saw her."

Gabe considered this. "Maybe so. Can you wait a sec?" He pulled a folded paper from his pack, scribbled hastily at the bottom, and refolded the note. "Um, I don't have any money for a stamp, and Mrs. Garvey says I'm not to go off on my own anyways. But I'll pay you back soon as I get a job. Can you mail this to Smitty? I just put in about Guppy."

When Mr. Boehm replied, "Of course," Gabe's face flickered with a quick smile and he ran off to math.

The next morning, at the start of English class, Gabe found on his desktop a small packet of blank envelopes, writing paper, and stamps, as well as Smitty's address at the Salem Veterans Affairs Medical Center. Gabe glanced secretly at Mr. Boehm, who was answering a long, involved question from Anneka.

An autumn storm marched through the mountains and towns of Virginia that week, cleaning the dust of Indian summer from the treetops and spattering mud onto sidewalks and the bottoms of picket fences. By Wednesday afternoon, the storm was wild. That evening, when he visited Gabe, Mr. Boehm asked Mr. and Mrs. Garvey to stay for the talk.

"Gabe, I have something important to discuss with you," Mr. Boehm began.

"Guppy's okay?"

"Yes, yes, she's getting better. It's not about Guppy. And Mr. Smith is fine, so far as we know."

Gabe fidgeted. "I know I didn't get my quiz signed."

"Quiz signed? No, it's not about school, either. It's about your uncle. And my father."

Gabe looked intently at his teacher as Mr. Boehm spoke. "I realize I haven't handled everything well—er, Monday comes to mind, and I suppose Sunday, too, but I really do need to tell you this, and I hope you're not upset. Your uncle, I understand from all the news reports, was a fine man and a superb soldier. He probably told you he was awarded the Purple Heart and the Distinguished Service Cross."

Gabe shook his head and Mr. Boehm continued. "I see. These are extremely high honors. And my father, somehow, my father, who is a senator from Connecticut, well, he has made arrangements to bury your uncle's body with other war heroes. At Arlington National Cemetery, near Washington, D.C. My parents called Monday night to tell me. I'll take you there; the funeral is on Saturday."

As Mr. Boehm spoke, Gabe's tongue began its rapid cheek movements. Mr. Boehm looked at Mrs. Garvey.

"What's bothering you, Gabe?" asked Mrs. Garvey.

Gabe looked down at his shoes and mumbled. "Uncle Vernon didn't know many people."

Mr. Boehm reassured him. "I think there will be a few. Anyway, it doesn't matter how many people come to a funeral. It's the love felt by the people there."

Gabe's tongue still roamed. "That ain't it."

"No?"

Gabe tried again, his head still bowed and his voice barely audible. "I'm scared of digging the hole."

Ulysses Garvey winked at his wife.

"No, no, Gabe," Mr. Boehm quickly assured him. "That's not how it works."

After his teacher explained what happened at a burial, Gabe asked: "But Guppy can't come?"

"That's right, Guppy can't come."

"And Webber?"

"I don't know if Webber will be allowed to come. I'll need to ask his mother."

"And Smitty?"

Here Mr. Boehm paused. "I don't think Smitty will come."

"Okay, then." Gabe looked up at Mr. Boehm. Gabe's cheeks were still. "You're nicer 'bout answering questions than Uncle Vernon," he said.

Mr. Boehm coughed a little and Mrs. Garvey asked him, with a rare smile, if he needed a glass of water.

The next evening, Thursday, even though the storm still raged, Mr. Boehm brought Guppy to the Garveys' enclosed back porch.

A wide smile arced across Gabe's face. He glanced over for permission from Mrs. Garvey, then tore out the back door. He nuzzled and hugged his beloved Guppy. He took her collar off and examined the stitches on her hind leg. Her tail thumped vigorously and she snuffled her happy snuffle. Gabe's fingers found the deep ruff between her shoulders. He talked nonstop.

"Oh, Guppy, Gup. You are the best dog there ever was. You're stronger than any old bullet. Didja miss me, girl? Huh? I sure missed you. A lot. And Smitty? Do you miss Smitty, too?"

Chapter 19

Saturday dawned cold and clear, with a brightness as gleaming as light dancing on beaten copper. Gabe, Mr. Boehm, Webber, and Mrs. Pickering, their suits and overnight bags stowed in the back of the Jeep with the boys, sailed over the ribbed Blue Ridge, heading northeast.

Webber teased Mr. Boehm along fifty miles of I-81 about the Friday class, in which students had had to present their group projects on *The Call of the Wild*. He gave a hilarious version of Anneka's performance. She had played John Thornton in her group's skit, and had been gripped in death's throes for a long, long time. Everyone would think she had finally died, when her quavering voice would rise again, calling for Buck.

"Well, how about you?" Mr. Boehm teased Webber. "I've never heard so much grunting in my life as I did when you were playing Buck trying to free the laden sled and its frozen runners."

"Yeah, didja hear Joaquin? 'The bathroom's down the hall, man.' But just be grateful Janet didn't get her way. She wanted us to play *Bachelorette,* with her as a she-wolf picking Buck from a lineup. But I reminded her that Gabe said he wouldn't play Buck, so she gave up."

Gabe looked at Webber in surprise. "When did that happen? She won't even talk to me."

"Oh, our group had a meeting one lunch. Monday, I think. You weren't there. She's bonkers for you, everyone knows that. Better you than me, Gabe-man."

Gabe looked out his window. Mrs. Pickering quickly changed the topic and wanted to know all about the senator.

"Remember, Webber," she cautioned for probably the hundredth time, "you're meeting a senator! Don't forget your manners. To think, we're staying in a senator's house! What was it like, Hank, growing up as the son of such an important man?"

Mr. Boehm said, "It was interesting," and busied himself with a lane change.

"Interesting, hmm?" Mrs. Pickering persisted. The backseat was perfectly quiet for once. Webber had even stopped bouncing his soccer ball on his knees.

"He's a politician," Mr. Boehm said at last. "Above all, he's a politician. It was—it was fine."

Gabe studied his teacher via the rearview mirror, but when Mr. Boehm glanced at the mirror they both quickly looked away.

After easing off Route 66, they ate lunch in a local inn's rustic dining room. Gabe and Mr. Boehm barely touched their food. In fact, only Webber had an appetite. Mrs. Pickering used the time to call home, checking on how her mother, her daughter, and the sitter were doing.

"Isn't Gabe handsome as a prince!" Mrs. Pickering commented after everyone changed clothes. The senator's office had sent a suit of clothes specially for Gabe to the Garveys' house.

Gabe clutched his new tie in his hand. Mr. Boehm tried to tie it around Gabe's neck as the boy stood stiffly, but Mr. Boehm couldn't do the reverse motions. So he tied it loosely around his own neck, transferred the tie to Gabe's, and gently cinched it. Gabe shuddered with the last tug—it felt like a noose! Like his nightmare!

"I don't want to go," he whispered desperately. It was all too final. Like the last page of a book. Or worse, the blank page after the last page. Could he ever think of his uncle as alive again? Would he always have to think of him so cold, so still?

"I know," Mr. Boehm told Gabe, "but it's better to go. It's a way to say goodbye."

"I don't want to say goodbye."

Mr. Boehm was silent. Then his face relaxed into a smile. "Hey, remember what Smitty said? He said we had to honor Uncle Vernon's memory. Remember? This is a way that we do that. Honoring Uncle Vernon as a man and as a soldier."

Gabe relaxed too. "Okay."

An hour later, they exited the George Washington Parkway onto Arlington National Cemetery's Memorial Drive. They were directed toward Patton's Circle, where services were to be held graveside. Gabe stared out of the car window. *So many gravestones! Rows and rows and rows.*

At the gravesite, Gabe was greeted by the officer in charge, the military chaplain, and Mr. Dillard, the funeral director, who told Gabe he had personally driven Vernon's body from the coroner's office. Gabe felt as if everything were a blur around him, as if he were on his tire swing, but instead of the swing moving, everything else was moving instead. By the time Senator Harry Boehm and Mrs. Ruth Boehm approached, Gabe felt numb.

"Hello, Mom, Father," said Mr. Boehm. "This is Gabe."

"Hello, dear Gabe," Mrs. Boehm said, kissing Gabe lightly on the cheek. "We're so sorry about your uncle, and to make you travel all this way. But it is lovely to meet you—Hank's told me such wonderful things."

Mrs. Boehm was tall and willowy, with long gray hair that she wore in a thick plait. Gabe was thinking about what she said, and so he barely got his hand out in time to shake the senator's hearty grip. Then, in the middle of the greeting, Gabe saw it—the dark rectangular hole that his uncle would be buried in.

Gabe couldn't take his eyes off the hole. It was surrounded by an artificial green carpet and topped by a gleaming metal frame. A frame, he was told, to hold the casket when it arrived.

There were lots of people. Some of the people were in uniform—one was in a motorized wheelchair. The senator, shaking hands in the crowd, was followed by many reporters with cameras and microphones. Gabe could see Mrs. Pickering straightening Webber's collar as he shook hands with Senator Boehm. Gabe felt a sudden urge to run.

But Mr. Boehm, who had not left his side, said, "Look, Gabe. There's someone you know."

"Hi, Ms. Rodriguez," said Gabe, brightening a little.

"Look at all these people," she commented.

"Who are they?" asked Gabe.

"They're calling themselves Friends of Sniffer. They've come from all over the country. I met a few. They said they heard about it on the news, but mostly through Internet Web sites for veterans. Some even brought their families."

"Oh!" said Gabe, and smiled for the first time.

Soon the color guard, caisson, and casket arrived, signaling the start of the ceremony. The casket was big and looked heavy. Dark, shiny wood with fancy metal handles. It was carried by uniformed soldiers with white gloves. The soldiers had rigid straight backs and buzz-cut hair. Their faces were set and their chins up. When they turned the casket, they moved in sharp, precise steps. They laid the casket on the frame and snapped a salute. The chaplain solemnly welcomed everyone, read from the Bible, and led the Lord's Prayer. Everyone stood and sat down together.

But Gabe, as he watched the ceremony, shivered at the thought that what was happening outside the casket seemed to have nothing to do with his uncle, who lay inside. Would Uncle Vernon be angry? Was he really in there? Would he start cussing in heaven? Just as Gabe started to tremble in nervousness, an unexpected voice rose from the back of the crowd.

"Excuse me, Chaplain, sir, if I may, I'd like to say a few words," said a man from the farthest row.

"Yes? Who are you?" asked the chaplain of the interrupter.

"PFC Gary O'Toole, sir, and—"

"Toolie!" shouted another man from the rear. Everyone twisted to see the speakers. When one of the pallbearers turned his head, he received such a glare from his commanding officer that he snapped back.

"Yes," Toolie admitted. "Anyway, I just wanted to say that Vernon Culligan is the reason I'm alive today, and I brought my son and wife all the way from Oklahoma City just to pay my respects. Thank you, Sniffer. That's all, Chaplain, thank you."

As the chaplain opened his mouth to continue, the man who had recognized Toolie spoke again.

"Thank you, Chaplain, sir. This is PFC Toby Sevren of Altoona, Pennsylvania. Better known as Tubby back then, 'cause I was thin as a rail. Not anymore! Anyway, I just wanted to add that when I was the you-know-what new guy, the cherry on the squad, it was Sniffer who took me under his wing and made sure I knew what was what. Otherwise, I'd have died that first day out. I almost picked up a discarded ration and he grabbed my hand in time. He was lightning quick, he was. The can was booby-trapped, of course. He sure could sniff out all those punji-stick traps, those mines, bouncing betties, and toe poppers the rest of us didn't see. Sniffer wasn't particularly friendly, but he sure looked out for me. Thanks, Sniffer. I never did thank you properly."

Gabe smiled at hearing "cherry" and rose slightly from his seat to get a better look at the real thing. Then he whispered to Mr. Boehm, "You and Smitty were right!"

Mr. Boehm smiled weakly.

"If that is all," began the chaplain, hoping to silence the crowd. But it wasn't all. These men were, after all, not in the service any longer. One by one, various men, from a range of races and backgrounds, ranks and careers, stood at their places and briefly told their tales. Of why they had to make this journey. Some of the stories were painful. Gabe learned about Vernon's last mission, the loss of his foot while rescuing three buddies as they came under friendly fire from above, the coordinates called in wrong by another squad. Gabe became very still and bowed his head.

The stories did seem, at last, to be at an end, until the African American officer in the wheelchair spoke. He sat very erect and his voice commanded authority.

"I would like the boy to read his essay. I knew Vernon Culligan. His nephew's essay would be the best tribute to Vernon."

The statement was met at first with silence, then with murmurs of approval. Gabe paled.

"My essay?" he asked Mr. Boehm.

"Yes, the one from the first week of school. It was found on your uncle's body, lying on his chest. And, well, the newspeople got hold of it somehow. It was in all the papers. They tried to interview me about it. Sorry, Gabe. I didn't want to tell you."

The ground beneath Gabe seemed to shift. He was speechless and he felt his heart pound.

"You don't have to read it, Gabe. That's okay. People will understand."

Gabe looked at Mr. Boehm and said, "I want to read it to Uncle Vernon. But I don't know if I can."

"Okay, here's what we'll do."

Several people waved newspaper clippings. After Mr. Boehm was handed a copy, he motioned for Gabe to stand on his chair, and they started reading together. At the end of the first paragraph, Mr. Boehm stopped, and Gabe continued alone.

"I want my uncle Vernon to know that I love him very much and that I'm sorry for all the trouble I caused. I want him to know that the tire swing we built makes me feel like I'm flying over miles and miles of countryside and the chestnut tree is always holding a pretty green umbrella over me. I want him to know that when I feel lonely I hear him talking in my head like he really is inside me. I want him to know that I will always be good and that way I won't ever have to go back to a foster home. I want Uncle Vernon to know that he is the best thing that ever happened to me." Gabe paused and added, "I love you, Uncle Vernon."

Slant light filtered through a nearby maple tree, adding a ruby glow to the gathering. The chaplain let the moment settle, then read a prayer. The ceremony ended with the rifle volley, the lonesome call of the bugler playing taps, and the folding of the flag by the pallbearers. As he presented the flag to Gabe, the next of kin, the chaplain spoke more gently than usual. "On behalf of a grateful nation, the president, and the United States Army, we present to you this flag, with our deepest sympathy and our greatest respect." After a moment he added, "Well done, soldier."

Chapter 20

Senator and Mrs. Boehm lived in the fanciest house Gabe had ever seen. The driveway to the house was long and circular, and tall white columns flanked the front door. Tables were laden with food for all who had attended the funeral. Webber started a soccer game on the lawn with some of the kids. But Gabe had been drawn to Captain Tarken, the veteran in the motorized chair. When Gabe found him, the captain was deep in conversation with Mr. Boehm.

"I can see that," Gabe heard the captain say, "but do you think the boy would want to—"

Seeing Gabe approach, Captain Tarken abruptly stopped

talking. Then the captain suggested that he and Gabe speak in private.

Mr. Boehm showed them into his father's study. Gabe sat opposite the captain at a small table. Captain Desmond Tarken had the thick neck and strong upper body of an athlete, and eyes that did not waver from the listener for a moment.

"Son, what do you know about the Vietnam War?" asked Captain Tarken.

"Um, Uncle Vernon said it was very far away, a long time ago, and the president of the United States told people to go there."

"Yes, Vietnam is far away, stretched out under China, roughly as long and skinny as the coastline from Maryland to Florida. The United States sent many men and women to help South Vietnam fight the North. The 1960s and '70s do seem like a time long ago, but for some people, they're just a heartbeat away." The captain paused. A vein on his forehead swelled for a moment; then he smiled. "I'll tell you what, let's fight a war, you and me. Do you play chess?"

"No, sir."

Captain Tarken began to teach Gabe the basic rules of chess on the senator's marble set. He taught Gabe how each chess piece could move, how to open a game and how not to open a game, in particular showing him the opening called the fool's mate.

"The king himself is weak; he would die if he led the attack. Yet you must be willing to sacrifice any member of your team to save the king. Vernon understood."

"He played chess?"

"No. He understood that the rules could kill you."

"Oh."

They made a couple of moves, the captain reminding Gabe of what was allowed.

"Tell me, Gabe, what are you going to do with yourself now that your secret is out?"

"I don't really know. They might . . ."

Captain Tarken frowned. His knight took one of Gabe's pawns. "They?" Gabe said nothing. The captain persisted. "I'm not asking 'them.' I'm asking *you*."

When Gabe still hesitated, Captain Tarken softened. "It's okay, son. It's okay to be afraid. They say there's no courage without fear. But you have to make sure that what you are afraid of isn't yourself. I'll tell you, many times we can't help those in need. But sometimes, some special times, the needs of two people match."

Gabe jumped at the sound of a knock. The door opened and Mr. Boehm ushered Ms. Rodriguez in.

"So sorry to interrupt," said Ms. Rodriguez, "but I couldn't leave without saying goodbye. Gabe?"

"Yes, ma'am," Gabe replied.

"I hope someday we can be friends and you won't get that panicked look when I walk into a room." She smiled and continued. "I know what's troubling you, what must be worrying you day and night. But before I go, I want to say one thing. I want you to know that people care about you. You're not alone. Do you understand?"

"Yessum."

"I remember that first day with your uncle Vernon, and you wouldn't even say what you liked to eat. A peanut butter and honey sandwich, wasn't it? Vernon may have been as crusty as a crab, but he knew from the very beginning how to teach you to express yourself. Remember that."

"Okay," said Gabe. "He was sorta crusty, wasn't he."

"Yes, we had our moments. But I didn't give him enough credit that night. And I didn't have enough confidence in myself. We're all still learning." She looked briefly toward Mr. Boehm, then looked back at Gabe. "Well, I'll be off now. Take care, Gabe."

"Ms. Rodriguez?"

"Yes, Gabe?"

"Thanks for finding Uncle Vernon for me."

Maria Rodriguez blushed slightly and quickly took her leave.

"I'll leave you two alone, then," said Mr. Boehm to the captain and Gabe.

"No, no," said Captain Tarken. "Please stay. We were just getting to Smitty, and I'd like you to hear as well."

Mr. Boehm pulled another chair up to the table. Gabe was already intently looking at the captain, concentrating on his every word.

"Smitty was with the platoon only a short time," Captain Tarken recounted. "It was 1968, after the Tet, when the North Vietnamese made a surprise attack on the South and even invaded the capital. Later that year, there were terrible riots in the United States Army prison at Long Binh. Tensions were high; morale was low. My company, B Company of the 1–52nd in the Americal—the 23rd Infantry Division—had many casualties. Vernon was on his third tour—he was a staff sergeant by then. Smitty

164

came in as radio telephone operator. He was bookish, one of the few privates to have finished college. He didn't fit in well. But then, nobody belonged there. Almost everyone wanted to go home. That's what some people didn't appreciate. You see, Vietnam taught all of us a few hard lessons. Because if the military didn't understand it before, the years in Vietnam definitely showed us that war isn't chess. A stalemate in chess is a draw. Nobody wins, but nobody loses. But a stalemate in war is different: everybody loses. You can't fight for a stalemate." A vein in Captain Tarken's forehead bulged. Then he continued.

"Back to our man, though. One evening we hit a sniper's house in a tiny village. While Vernon stood lookout, he sent Smitty into the hut to check that we got him, which we had. But there was more gunfire inside, and Vernon ran in ready to fire. When they both came out, Smitty was shaken. He wouldn't talk. It was as if he had turned to stone; you couldn't even see him blink. I don't think I'll ever forget that look. Vernon said Smitty would no longer be any good to the squad. Vernon had a sense about people; even the locals trusted him. So I sent Smitty to the back. A soldier who wouldn't shoot was no good in the field. He eventually was transferred to Graves Registration at Tan Son Nhut, where they process remains for shipment stateside. Nasty business, the bodies, the stench—I'd rather not go into it. But I would like to tell you what went on in the hut. Do you want to hear it?"

Gabe clutched the edge of the table. "Yes," he said hoarsely. "Smitty said he had a secret."

"I expect he has more than one. But that may be the

one that haunts him the most. And this is one reason I wanted Mr. Boehm here. Vernon did, eventually, tell me what went on in that hut. Remember the fool's mate in chess I warned you about, Gabe? That you can get set up for the easiest trap and not realize it until it's too late? It was like that all the time in the war. We were set up, trapped, conned over and over. It made you suspicious of the slightest movement. It made you jumpy, and sometimes you'd overreact."

Gabe nodded, thinking of the November night when his uncle tossed him under the truck bed. "Yes," he said.

"That's what happened in the hut. The sniper was dead, but Smitty saw something move in a dark corner and he fired at it. Over and over. It could have been another sniper."

"Did Uncle Vernon shoot it?"

"No, Vernon ran in and saw what it was. Vernon was a very keen soldier, incredible instincts. He told Smitty to hold his fire."

Captain Tarken paused and glanced at Mr. Boehm. "Gabe seemed very curious to know about Vernon and Smitty," Tarken explained.

"I understand," said Mr. Boehm.

"Good," said the captain. "I'll proceed. It wasn't a sniper, as you probably guessed. It was a young boy, maybe ten years old. There was a gun at his side. Kids younger than that would shoot at you, or set booby traps. But when I read in the paper this week what Smitty had done to himself some years ago, well, I'm sure this is why."

Gabe had stiffened in his chair.

"You know what happened?" asked the captain.

"I think so," whispered Gabe.

"Well, you're right. He had killed the boy; most of the shots had hit his face. Believe me, worse things happened in that war, but I doubt Smitty thinks so."

"But—but it wasn't his fault," said Gabe.

"That's exactly right, Gabe. *It wasn't his fault.*" Captain Tarken paused to let his words sink in. Looking directly into Gabe's eyes, he continued: "But sometimes you blame yourself for things that aren't your fault."

Gabe lowered his head.

"Gabe," said Mr. Boehm. "Listen to me. Your uncle's death wasn't your fault. It wasn't anyone's fault. It just happened, that's all."

Mr. Boehm looked over at Captain Tarken. "Thank you," he said.

The captain nodded. "It's hard to live, sometimes, with all the things life throws at you."

"You're right," agreed Mr. Boehm. A silence settled in the room. Gabe had withdrawn into his chair. It was all so unfair. No wonder Uncle Vernon got mad when Gabe asked him about killing anyone. *They were people! Real people!*

"Life is a 'puppet thing,' " said Gabe suddenly. Both Mr. Boehm and Captain Tarken looked at him in surprise.

"Did your uncle tell you that?" asked Captain Tarken.

"No," replied Gabe. "That's from a book Mr. Boehm assigned. What my uncle said was"—and here Gabe looked sheepishly back and forth between the men—" 'scum-lickin' pus-suckin' buckets of trouble ken happen.' "

"Yes, that does sound more like the Vernon I knew," said Captain Tarken, and gave a soft chuckle.

After a moment, the captain spoke again. "I've learned some things in my life, and I've decided to share them with you both. You may not want me to, but as a black officer in a wheelchair, I'll take my chances. Here they are: one, life is short; two, life is precious; and three, communication is key."

Gabe again sat straight, listening carefully to each word.

"What do you think, Gabe, that Ms. Rodriguez was saying to you?" asked the captain.

"I, um . . ."

"Remember, life is short and precious, and communication is key."

"She said that I'm not alone."

"That's right, very good. And to express yourself. So, Gabe, it's your move. I'll ask you again, what are you going to do with yourself?"

Gabe hesitated.

Mr. Boehm leaned forward and said, "Perhaps, Captain, he's not ready. He's been through so much already. I wouldn't want—"

Captain Tarken calmly stopped Mr. Boehm by holding up a hand. "Shall I ask Mr. Boehm to leave the room?" the captain asked Gabe.

"No, please, no," said Gabe.

Gabe could feel Mr. Boehm looking intently at him. But when Mr. Boehm began, "Gabe, I—" Captain

Tarken again interrupted by holding up the palm of his hand.

"Why not, Gabe?" persisted the captain.

"Because, because . . ." Gabe's voice was pressured. He felt as if air couldn't escape his chest and he was ready to burst.

"Say it," Captain Tarken said firmly.

"Because, because I need him!" Gabe shouted. He flinched. *What have I done?* But when Gabe opened his eyes he saw a broad smile on the captain's face. Gabe followed where the captain was looking and saw Mr. Boehm wiping the corner of his eye.

"Gabe, I need you, too," Mr. Boehm said. "I . . . I don't have a wife or kids. That just hasn't gone my way. Yet I believe that raising a child is the most important experience one can have in life. Every time I've visited my sisters and their families, I've desperately wished that one of my nieces or nephews were my kid. Then you appeared in my classroom. The day you picked *Of Mice and Men* from the shelf and started reading in class, and every day since, I realized you were the kid I'd love to take to family gatherings. *As my kid.* But of course, I didn't understand then what had happened to you. Later, I talked with Ms. Rodriguez, who said that at your age, if there's more than one option, it would be up to you."

"More than one option?" asked Gabe.

"Sure, it's just not the exact right time for her, but don't forget Mrs. Pickering."

"But she'll never need me . . ."

". . . the way that I need you."

"What do you know—a match where everyone wins," said Captain Tarken. "Well, I must be off. No need to show me out."

When Mr. Boehm had finished shaking the captain's hand and thanking him over and over, Gabe jumped from his chair and did something he couldn't remember ever doing before. He leaned in to Captain Tarken and gave him a hug.

"Hey, Gabe," said Mr. Boehm. "I'm famished. How about we go raid the kitchen for some peanut butter, honey, and bread?"

"Sure, Mr. Boehm!"

"It's Hank, Gabe. You can call me Hank."

"Wow." Gabe grinned, then added, "I can't wait to tell Smitty."

Chapter 21

Five weeks and a day after the funeral, Gabe stood with Hank Boehm at number 13 Lapan Lane. The air held the faint scent of raked leaves burning, or perhaps hickory ash rising from a distant chimney. Every Sunday, just before noon, Gabe insisted on visiting his old home, which was now held for him in trust. He didn't want to go on Saturdays, because of the Saturday postman. Guppy, who had never liked men in uniform, had become even more easily angered by them since the shooting. Otherwise, she was in good spirits, obeyed Gabe instantly, and slept, bathed, and played with him. She had the slightest limp when running. Tiresias could not run as fast as Guppy, and his poor eyesight made him wary of rapid motions. But the dogs were at least companions.

In the weeks since the funeral, Gabe had been writing to two people, but only one of the correspondents wrote back. This was Janet. She was tongue-tied and embarrassed when she tried to talk to him, but she and Gabe left notes for each other in their backpacks. Her letters were decorated with multicolored inks and stickers, all of which Gabe saved.

The person who didn't write back was Smitty. Gabe often reread Smitty's earlier cards, particularly those about Guppy. Twice a week, Gabe mailed a brief note to Smitty at the Salem VA hospital. Gabe knew that Smitty was still a patient there; Mr. Dillard had said so to Hank. Smitty was free to come and go as he pleased, but Mr. Dillard said that although Smitty was welcome to come back to work, he had only returned once, to pick up some clothes.

Over and over in his notes, Gabe said he understood that Guppy belonged to Smitty, and that if Smitty missed having her, he could leave a note in the mailbox. Gabe told Smitty he would collect mail Sundays at noon, and would release Guppy to the far side of the ravine if Smitty wanted his dog back. It was the only plan Gabe could think of.

So each Sunday Gabe collected the mail and checked the house. Then he and Hank would walk with the dogs under the trees. Sometimes Gabe would swing on his tire under the shedding chestnut tree; Hank had tried it a couple of times as well. Then Gabe would sigh and they would return in Hank's Jeep to their new home—a rental cottage they had selected together. Gabe's room held his desk and a new trundle bed. Webber, still annoyed about sharing his room with his sister, enjoyed weekend sleepovers.

During this time, all the sheriff's holdings were delivered to Gabe, including the fan button, which had been collected for fingerprinting. The only contents of the locked fire box were Vernon's honorable discharge papers from the army; a single photograph of Gabe, smiling on Mrs. Pickering's front stoop; and Gabe's adoption documents. Gabe's adoption by Hank was not yet finalized, but their case was scheduled on Judge Garvey's docket for the following summer.

On this Sunday, the air was cold and the sky hoary and thick with coming winter. A pile of curled dry leaves had collected by the mailbox. Gabe took a deep breath and opened the curved metal door. Then he swallowed hard. There, inside the rusted box, next to a couple of stray letters addressed to Vernon Culligan, was the deep green envelope that had always filled Gabe with hope and dread. His hand shook as he removed the letter from the box.

"This is it," he said unsteadily to Hank.

Gabe opened the envelope and removed the cream-colored card.

> *Never straight, our paths are also rarely*
> *   unforked.*
> *I have thought about your kind offer night*
> *   and day.*
> *The answer is . . .*

Gabe's hand trembled as he turned the card over.

I will wait, as you suggest, then depart.

"Oh!" cried Gabe. "He's waiting for Guppy! I need to write him a note. Come on, inside, quick!"

Gabe ran into the house while the dogs continued to snuffle through the fallen leaves. He went straight to his uncle's old study and opened drawers till he found a piece of paper. He knocked the pencil holder over in his haste, and scribbled a note on the paper.

"I need—" Gabe continued, "I know what to do!"

He ran into the kitchen and found some string. Then he tore through the dog door, almost somersaulting in his hurry.

"Here, Guppy, come here, quick!"

Gabe feverishly folded his note, then tied it securely to Guppy's collar—a collar with tags that Hank had insisted she wear.

"Come on! Let's go!" shouted Gabe. He headed toward the trees.

"Where are we going?" asked Hank, sprinting to catch up. While Tiresias remained behind, nosing in the brittle leaves, Guppy, Gabe, and Hank ran over trees' molt and through the brisk air.

At the edge of the ravine, Gabe knelt, rubbed Guppy's fur backward up her spine, then hugged her, digging his hands into the thick ruff above her shoulders. He puffed into the soft fur behind her ears and spoke earnestly to her. He could feel tears start to burn his eyes.

"He needs you now, Guppy, more'n I need you. You're his anyway. You always were. I love you, Guppy. You're the best dog there ever was. Now go, go on, get out of here. He's waiting for you. Go!"

Gabe stood and released his hold. He pointed across the chasm.

"Go on, girl. Good girl."

Guppy stood at the edge, uncertainly looking at Gabe. She gazed across the ravine and held her nose to the air. Then she leaned her heavy bulk against his body, nuzzled his hand, and loped easily down the gully, across the wooden plank, and up the other side. She hesitated once, on the far side. Gabe again held out his arm, pointing to the distance. His voice was less a command than a plea.

"Go, Guppy. Go find Smitty."

Guppy turned and quickened her stride as she entered the brush between the trees. They could hear her footfalls over a patch of dry leaves, the crackle of small twigs breaking, and then nothing. Gabe felt as if a piece of his body had been carved out of him.

"That was a brave and generous thing to do," said Hank. He knelt by Gabe. "I'm proud of you."

A broken V of migrating geese flew overhead in the gauzy midday. Their honking spread through the air and dispersed like dust.

And then, from behind a stand of trees, a man appeared. Smitty wore a broad hat with a low brim and flaps to the shoulders. He was a slight man, but his gait was steady. He stopped at the edge of the ravine, directly across from Gabe and Hank. Smitty bowed his head and slowly removed his hat, which he held with one hand before his chest. He raised his head and looked at Gabe. One side of his face was particularly misshapen and caved in: Gabe saw the shrunken, pocked pull of scars, the patchwork of multihued skin grafts, and a missing eye. Smitty's mouth was lopsided like a sideways comma.

"Smitty!" Gabe cried, starting to scramble down, over the dirt and rock rim.

But Smitty held up a hand and said, "No, Gabe, please." His voice was slightly garbled, and he repeated, "No," firmly to make sure Gabe understood. Gabe backed up the embankment. The air was still.

"Hello, Mr. Smith," said Hank, and bowed slightly.

"A pleasure to meet you, Mr. Boehm," replied Smitty. "I have something for Gabe, and I wanted to give it to him in person this time. I hope you forgive me."

"There is nothing to forgive," Hank said.

"Thank you." Smitty made a low clicking sound, and Guppy came bounding from the trees, ran to his side, and promptly sat. He reached down and gave her a pat.

"She is yours, Gabe," said Smitty. "Please accept her as a gift from my heart to your most generous soul."

Smitty looked down at Guppy, and held her head between his hands. She looked directly at him as he made a series of clicks. When he released her, she rubbed her flank against his leg, then charged down the divide and up to Gabe. Gabe gleefully rubbed her ears and jowls, but, glancing up, noticed Smitty turning toward the trees.

"No, wait!" Gabe's voice rose, shrill and desperate. "Thank you, but can I see you again? Please. Smitty! Please don't go!"

Smitty took a few steps, then paused, still poised to leave. After several moments and another call from Gabe, he turned back. "Gabe," said Smitty slowly, "life is difficult for me. Even in our friendship, Vernon and I never met like this. You have accepted me without question, Gabe, and for this I am eternally humbled. I live my life one day at a time. Perhaps already in your life you have experienced this, and you can understand. I do not know what the future holds, but this I do know: I would not have survived the loss of Vernon for even a day if it had not been for you."

With that statement, Smitty swiftly turned, put on his hat, and strode away.

"Smitty!" Gabe called to Smitty's retreating back.

Gabe felt hollow. He stared hard across the gap of the ravine, as if the earth's rift had shifted into a new, more dangerous pattern. To steady himself, he dug his fingers deep into Guppy's ruff, and, kneeling by the dog, wrapped his arms around her neck. Hank joined them. His words of comfort rippled like soft breezes fluttering through leaves. But Hank's efforts were interrupted by Gabe's sharp intake of air. The boy had discovered, tucked and tied under Guppy's collar, a small note. With shaking hands, Gabe removed and unfolded the paper. With Hank, Gabe read Smitty's perfect calligraphic script.

Gabe,
A life marked only by secrets is of little
    consequence.
If I have helped one child toward happiness
    in helping you, then my life has, after all,
    been worth living.
                    With deepest gratitude,

Gabe looked at Hank, then turned over the card. A small mark lay perfectly centered on the paper. The script was exquisite and of the tiniest size. Gabe held the card close to his face, and squinted with one eye to read the signature:

                  Paul